Lásko

Lásko

a novel

Catherine Cooper

Freehand Books acknowledges the financial support for its publishing program provided by the Canada Council for the Arts and the Alberta Media Fund, and by the Government of Canada through the Canada Book Fund.

The author acknowledges the support of the Canada Council for the Arts' Explore and Create Programme. *Lásko* is a work of fiction. With the exception of certain public figures and historical events, the events and characters are not intended to portray actual events or individuals, and the opinions expressed should not be considered or construed as representing the author's.

Freehand Books
515–815 1st Street sw Calgary, Alberta T2P 1N3
www.freehand-books.com

Book orders: UTP Distribution
5201 Dufferin Street Toronto, Ontario M3H 5T8
Telephone: 1-800-565-9523 Fax: 1-800-221-9985
utpbooks@utpress.utoronto.ca utpdistribution.com

Library and Archives Canada Cataloguing in Publication
Title: Lásko / Catherine Cooper.
Names: Cooper, Catherine, 1982– author.
Identifiers: Canadiana (print) 20230454275 | Canadiana (ebook) 20230454283 | ISBN 9781990601347 (softcover) | ISBN 9781990601361 (PDF) | ISBN 9781990601354 (EPUB)
Classification: LCC PS8605.O654 L37 2023 | DDC C813/.6—DC23

Edited by Deborah Willis
Book design by Natalie Olsen
Cover paint texture © FreshBackgrounds / Shutterstock.com
Printed on FSC® recycled paper and bound in Canada by Imprimerie Gauvin

for my sisters

Love, oh love, where do you come from?

You do not grow in the garden.

You are not sown in the field.

I am not sown in the field.

I give birth to myself.

Between men and maidens

I am walking.

TRADITIONAL MORAVIAN

Spring

2015

JUNE'S FINAL MESSAGE says, *Will be at station. Am fat. Have white hair.* But the woman who meets me in Český Krumlov is tall and slender with grey hair, so I spend the drive to her house wondering if something dreadful is going to happen to me, because why would someone lie like that?

June and her husband Pieter are recluses. She used the word herself in her first message to me. They've lived in the Czech Republic for over twenty years, but they don't leave their property except to shop, bring their dog to the vet, and take their annual trip to Spain.

In the pictures on the housesitting website, their "estate" looked elegant and romantic, if slightly run down. In reality, it's derelict. Pieter meets us in the driveway. Behind him is a tractor with three white spotlights beaming from its grill although it's midday.

"Skin and bones," he says, looking me up and down. "Come on, then." He moves toward the tractor.

June says, "Let her have a cup of tea first."

"Princess is up for some work, isn't she?" He was probably handsome once. June is so regally beautiful that it's hard to imagine what kind of disaster could have caused her to end up here, with him.

I open the back door of June's Jeep to get my suitcase, but Pieter shoos me away. *I know you,* I think when he pushes in front of me and picks up the heavy bag like it's nothing. *I've known hundreds of yous.*

I reach for my computer bag. "I can take that, thanks."

"What kind of accent is that?" he asks.

"Canadian, but I've moved around a lot."

He seems to be preparing another question, but June interrupts. "Come and meet Sarie," she says.

Pieter says, "Speaking of mongrels."

I follow June up the gravel driveway, past rusty farm equipment, an empty swimming pool bordered by a thicket of bare bushes, and a ten-foot structure swathed in blankets and emitting a cacophony of bird sounds.

On the other side of their home's ornate wooden front door is a cavernous room that smells of wet dog and fried meat. There's a kitchen in the far corner, a wooden dining table and chairs, a few old sofas around a huge TV, a woodstove, and a four-poster bed whose faded white canopy is stained with what I assume is cooking fat.

A black dog leaps from under the blankets, jumps on me, and licks my face while June says, "Sarie, no," without conviction.

"Get down, man," Pieter bellows from the doorway, and the dog slinks back to bed.

"That's our baby," June says. She tucks the whimpering animal in under the covers.

"So?" Pieter is silhouetted in the doorway, his feet spread and his arms crossed. Looking at him makes me feel desperate to be alone, check my emails, and sleep.

14

THE MISSION IS to collect firewood for me to use while they're gone. I tell them I'll be fine with my hot water bottle, but they insist. In the forest, as Pieter sections the wood with a chainsaw and June and I load the pieces onto the trailer, it occurs to me that no one knows where I am. I didn't give Gina or Becca an address, and I kept my plans from Drew, because I don't want him making any grand romantic gestures.

On the way back to the house, the tractor gets stuck in the mud. Pieter tries to get it out by lifting it with the attachment fixed to the front. He drives the attachment into the ground and revs the motor. June's eyes shift between him, me, and the door. When he accelerates, the front of the cab lifts off the ground, so the tractor is leaning back. We're out of the mud, but it isn't clear how he's going to move the tractor forward.

"Shit!" he shouts. He seems about to give us some instructions when June reaches past me and flips the handle on the cab door. Pieter bellows, "No!" as the door swings open and slams against the side of the tractor, shattering the window and sending chunks of glass skittering under my feet.

"What the fuck are you doing, treasure?" he shouts. For a moment I think he's going to hit her. Instead, he smashes his fist against the side of the tractor, and some of the glass still clinging to the top of the window frame falls onto her lap. I turn away and tuck my face into my armpit to hide my nervous laughter.

"I thought . . ." she says.

"You weren't thinking, man!"

She rests her hand on my shoulder. It must look like I'm crying. Pieter's feet make a sucking sound when he lands in the mud. June and I climb through the broken glass and silently follow him back to the house. When we arrive, he's already left, and I'm relieved to have a break from his presence.

At sunset he comes tearing down the driveway with the trailer of wood bouncing behind the Jeep. June and I wrap up the strange, circular conversation we've been having, during which a few things have become clear: Number one, the wood is not for me. It's for the dog, who has to be kept warm at all times. June tells me this over and over again. The fire *has* to be going all the time, and every time Sarie gets up, she *has* to be tucked back in. Number two, Pieter and June probably expect me to sleep in the dog's bed, because it seems like the main room is the only habitable room in the house, and the dog's bed is the only bed in there. I'm not sure where they expect me to sleep until they leave. And number three, they don't seem to have any plans to leave.

After dinner, which I slyly feed to Sarie under the table, Pieter teaches me how to make the fire using teabags soaked in kerosene, then June shows me to a room in a separate, unused wing of the house. We have to move several large pieces of furniture and cross a wooden plank bridging a hole in the floor to get there, and the room smells musty, so I have to open all of the windows despite the cold, but I'm so happy to be alone that I don't care. I'm amazed to find the wifi signal is strong, and I stay up until two a.m. reading and refreshing my emails.

I'M SITTING BY the pool on a lounge chair that seems to be made entirely of rust, reading a book I found in a pile next to my bed. It has one of those busy sci-fi covers with embossed metallic lettering, but it's actually kind of interesting. According to the author, after diverging from the last ancestor we share with apes, our hominid predecessors evolved for millions of years without using symbols or innovating beyond iterations on a basic stone toolkit. Then roughly 100,000 years ago, many millennia after we developed anatomically modern brains, our symbol-making capacity mysteriously and suddenly (in relative terms) activated, reaching a turning point about 40,000 years ago, when our Stone Age ancestors started leaving evidence of advanced artistic, religious, and cultural behaviour.

I'm surprised I've never heard of this before, but if it's true, it's such an interesting question. Maybe it's the most interesting question. What makes us *us*? So far the author is talking about contact with psychoactive plants, but I have a feeling the answer is going to have something to do with aliens.

"Snack?" June is carrying a tray of cold cuts, olives, crackers, and cheese arranged in a fan shape on a silver platter. I tell her I've already had breakfast. I'm not wearing makeup, and I search her face for a reaction to the constellation of pink scars on my cheek.

"I shouldn't eat this either," she says, pinching her waist. "What did you have?"

"I had some protein bars in my suitcase."

She looks disgusted, which is rich considering the state of her house.

Pieter arrives wielding an electronic fly swatter in the shape of a tennis racket. I can feel him coming before I see him, but it's too late to get up and pretend I have something else to do. He seizes a handful of meat from June's tray. "Princess won't eat this rubbish, will she?" he says.

He sits sideways on the recliner, facing me on my scarred side. June puts her tray down at the end of his seat and perches on the round wrought iron table next to him. I wonder if they're trying to be polite. I consider telling them that I prefer to be left alone, as I assume they do, but then a terrible possibility occurs to me. They're enjoying having someone else around. They are putting off leaving *because* I'm here.

The pool is empty apart from the layer of leaves and other dead matter on the bottom, which cover a Tibetan mandala June insists I will love. I guess they think I'm a Buddhist because I don't eat meat. Pieter practically forces me to use a stick to move some leaves aside so I can see the faded tiles underneath, and something about it makes me feel so lonely.

"Not even a cracker?" June says as soon as I sit down again.

"I try to avoid wheat."

"Do these have wheat?"

"I don't know."

"Are you allergic?"

"I haven't been well," I say. I wish she would stop.

"What's wrong with you?"

"I had an illness."

"What kind of illness?"

"I took antibiotics for a year, and since then I've had some issues, so I have to be careful what I eat."

"You think antibiotics made you sick?" I know what she's thinking. I'm a hypochondriac. Picky eater. Princess. I used to think the same thing about people like me.

"Yes."

"Why do you think that?"

"Because it's not good to take them for a year."

"What were they for?"

"Malaria."

"Antibiotics for malaria?"

"Yes."

"Did it work?"

"No."

"So why did he prescribe them?"

"He was a she," I say. "And I don't know."

"What about whole-wheat crackers?" she says. I'm going to try ignoring her. "Mája?" she says, incorrectly. This is one of the reasons why I spell my pen name with a y. "It's *Mája*," I say. "Like papaya."

"Oh no! Why didn't you say something sooner? I don't think I can change it now." I don't respond, and a brief silence ensues. Normally, I fill silences with questions. My father calls me inquisitorial, but studying people is my job insofar as I have one. I'm

LÁSKO

not interested in turning June and Pieter into characters, though.
I just want them to go away.

"What about whole-wheat crackers?" June says again.

"No, thank you."

"I think I have some with flax in them. Will you eat those?"

"No, thanks."

"What about . . ."

"Oh give over," Pieter says. "It's up to her if she wants to
destroy herself." I feel like he's looking at my scars when he says
this, and I want to turn to him wide-eyed and scream, but instead
I open my laptop, hoping they will take the hint.

I enter my password and wait for my emails to load, but
there's only one from Drew with the subject, "Please don't do
this." Nothing else.

"I had a dentist who hummed," Pieter says. I don't look up
from my screen. "He had this fucking thing in my mouth, so I
couldn't comment on his performance. When it was over, I told
him, *Next time I'll have it without the musical accompaniment.*"

It's hopeless. I close my computer. "Was I humming?"

"Yes."

I ask if they have children.

"Pieter has . . ." June says.

"Two sons," he interrupts. "But I don't think much of them.
One's a bullshitter, and the other one is really weird. Doesn't look
you in the eye."

I already feel the urge to open my laptop and refresh my
emails again. I'm like one of those lab mice that will push the
lever in its cage hundreds of times to get a hit of cocaine.

"Just because we're related doesn't mean we have to love each
other," Pieter says. "I told my sons that when they were children."

I won't give him the satisfaction of looking appalled.

"Because when you have children, you get this thing that's
not you and not the other person. It's another thing altogether.

And who says you're going to like that thing? Who says you have to?"

"Sure," I say.

"The fact is that when you have a child, there's a good chance you're creating a monster," he continues. I want to say, *You're the fucking monster, dude.* He carries on. "You can give the birds lettuce once a day, but only . . ."

"Iceberg." We've been over this.

"They don't *like* any other kind!" he shouts.

"If you need anything, you can always go to the farmer's house," June says.

"You won't need anything," Pieter says. "And if you do, you can call us."

"But if you can't reach us, you can go to the farmer. It's not far."

Pieter kicks her shin hard enough to make her wince. "I don't want him to know she's *here*, treasure."

Now they have my interest. "Why?" I ask.

"He likes women," June says.

"And he likes them skin and bones, like you." Pieter whips his swatter in front of my face. There's a popping sound. "On the wing!" he shouts. "Ten points! Of course you'll disapprove, but I don't care. I'll kill them all."

"Don't be afraid," June says. "The farmer is harmless."

"You're giving her the wrong idea," Pieter says. "Men are men. But I wouldn't dream of going near someone like her, because . . ."

"I'd kill you if you did," June says.

"And neither would he," Pieter says. "Because he has a wife, and Czech women are very good around the home."

I'm going to leave that alone, not try, as I usually do, to compensate for other people's social inadequacies by pretending their behaviour is normal.

When they've finished eating, June drives me to Český Krumlov and shows me how to shop for food. "Penny Market is best for deals, Lidl is my favourite overall, and Tesco is also good, but too big for me," she says. "If they ask questions at the check-out, just say ne. It means no."

"What are they asking?"

"I don't know. Just say ne."

I want to ask her how it's possible that she's lived in the Czech Republic for over twenty years and can't speak more than one word of the language, but I'm in no position to judge. I lived with my mother for seven years, and I only managed to retain one Czech phrase: mluviti stříbro, mlčeti zlato. Speaking is silver, silence is golden.

I WAKE UP, reach for my computer, and refresh Gmail. One email from my aunt, Gina:

> Sweetheart,
>
> How are you? I've heard nothing.
>
> I'll be off on Thursday for a ten-day Vipassana retreat. Would like to chat beforehand. I will give you a try on Skype tomorrow. I believe you are twelve hours behind.
>
> I'm holding you in white light. Remember you are guided, and you are loved.
>
> Auntie Gina

Her email signature is the quote from Marianne Williamson about our greatest fear being our own immeasurable power. My aunt has a quote for every situation, but her favourites are "until you make the unconscious conscious, it will direct your life, and you will call it fate" and "as soon as you decide to change something, the universe offers you a test." For as long as I can remember, she's been using this pair of adages as a completely satisfying explanation for why life is hard and bad things happen: you invited it by wanting something, or you invited it by not wanting something. Either way, you brought it on yourself.

I click on an email from Drew. It's a photo collage of us over the years. I won't respond. Any kindness from me is only going to make it worse.

My troubles, as he called them, didn't come on suddenly. One day I was happy and fine, the next I felt hopeless and desperate to escape. After a year of perfect skin thanks to daily broad-spectrum antibiotics, I'd started getting acne on my left cheek, always before my period. Then, right around the time the shaking wall hallucinations started, my period stopped altogether. My writing career, if you could call it that, had also dried up, and my income—cobbled together from a combination of contracting as a marketing and communications coordinator for a community college and writing content for online magazines for per-word rates that amounted to about two cents an hour—barely covered my half of the expenses and my student loan payments.

At first I thought my symptoms stemmed from anxiety about taking concrete steps to settle down with Drew. I considered looking for a short-term contract overseas, but I'd only recently come back from Sierra Leone, I couldn't justify going away again so soon, and more importantly, I couldn't keep doing work I don't believe in any more.

When I chose to study international development, I imagined myself helping people, not writing about them, and when I allowed life to corral me toward communications, I found that to a disturbing degree words were the whole point. Analyses and objectives became strategies, initiatives, messaging, reports, newsletters, fundraising stories, which became more money, more strategies, more messaging, more paper, more words. I know those initiatives helped some individuals, and they gave other individuals, like me, jobs, but I didn't see them improving anything on a systemic level, and the more I learned, the more convinced I became that they may be doing the opposite.

I've written poetry since I was a child, but I was in my mid-twenties before I tried writing fiction. The day after I wrote my first short story (all in one sitting, never happened since), I went to a party where I struck up a conversation with an author I admire. When I mentioned the story, she offered to read it, and I was stunned when she wrote back that it "irradiates the reader with emotion" and offered to show it to the editorial board she sat on at a prestigious literary magazine. After it was published, I was contacted by a literary agent, and then momentum took over to a certain extent, but when I finally decided to commit to the insecure, trickle-fed life of an artist, the momentum ran out. Now I've asked for so many extensions on the edits for my second novel that the publisher has threatened to take back my puny advance.

It's not that I don't want to do the edits. I can't. I see things differently than I did when I wrote the first draft, but I haven't settled on a new way of seeing, and despite my writer self's attraction to the subjects that inspire the greatest shame and trepidation in my soul, I'm actually terrified of being criticised or causing harm or offense, so when I consider how much I now see I got wrong, I'm sure that no matter what I write I'll end up regretting it for reasons I haven't considered yet and will possibly never understand. Maybe I would mind more if I hadn't already resigned myself to being mediocre and tired of trying, but as it is, in some ways it feels like a relief to think that I could just give up.

I started a dream journal, hoping that would help, but instead it triggered the return of the nightmares I used to have after my mother disappeared. I call them something-is-coming dreams. Usually I'm trying to escape from an invisible threat by unsuccessfully packing or locking myself into a house where none of the windows or doors work. Other themes include attempting to appease psychopaths by being adorable and being chased in public but unable to scream or ask for help.

The something-is-coming dreams aren't as gruesome as some of my other nightmares, but they're much more disturbing. I also think they're connected to the shaking walls, because every time I have one, I hallucinate the shaking walls shortly after I wake up.

One night I dreamt I was being hunted by people who owned me, and when they caught me they forced me to cut a baby out of my womb and give it to them. I woke up to the shaking walls, and when it was over, I found that the sheets under me were soaked in black blood.

Drew took me to emergency. They did some tests, and the doctor told me I might have cervical cancer and the bleeding could be a sign it had spread to surrounding tissue. We stopped at Tim Hortons on the way home so I could buy a dozen honey crullers, and I sat in the bath for hours, bleeding, eating donuts, grieving the children I would probably never have as I looked at my skin pucker in the water and pondered what it would look like when I was dead.

I emailed my editor to ask for yet another extension and spent the next week in bed watching reality TV with noise-cancelling headphones, entering contests with travel prizes, signing up for European housesitting websites, applying for writing residencies, doing online personality quizzes with titles like What Should I Be When I Grow Up? Drew tried to be supportive. He kept coming into the bedroom and asking if I was okay. I wanted to scream, *No, I'm not! I'm dying!* Instead I said, "Yes, thanks," and put my headphones back on.

According to the test results, I was okay, or at least I didn't have cervical cancer. My GP said the blood was just "left over" from my last period, and she put the shaking walls down to stress. She referred me to a psychiatrist.

I did some research on my own, and following my sojourn in bed, I put myself on a strict programme to sort out my gut flora and hormones, cutting out grains, dairy, and sugar, and taking daily doses of omega-3, milk thistle, and three kinds of probiotic, including a soil-based one and a beneficial yeast. I felt briefly energised by this project. I was going to solve my problem by following advice from people on the internet. It was going to get better.

It got much worse. My research told me to expect that. It's called die-off. My skin was worse than ever, but I soldiered on. Then it stopped. The scars were still there, but my skin stopped breaking out. My dreams changed, too. The something-is-coming dreams were replaced by dreams in which I'd had a baby and forgotten about it and had to find it. I knew it would be grim, because the baby would be starved and covered in shit and possibly dead. My aunt told me it was about me neglecting my calling.

Sometimes I dreamt I'd given birth, and I was in the hospital, alone and ambivalent. I'd try to call Drew, but the phone would be all mixed up—the number one was the letter P, two was a green triangle, and so on. I felt like my body had been hijacked, and I didn't belong to myself any more. That feeling crept more and more into my waking life, too, until I was spending most of my time thinking of ways to escape. But from what? Drew had just been promoted to associate professor, we were planning to buy a house, we had a great group of friends, and it was a miracle I'd ended up with someone so stable and normal and *nice*, all things considered. I should have been happy. I wanted to be happy. But none of my usual strategies worked.

I looked into training to be a counsellor—I doubt I'm the first lost soul to have this idea—but after the head of the programme I was considering welcomed a class of prospective students by writing *liberal humanist* and *social constructionist* on the whiteboard and telling us, "Now you think like this," point-ing at liberal humanist, "At the end of this programme," sliding her laser pointer over to social constructionist, "You're going to think like this," I decided not to take out another student loan to find out how she planned to pull that off.

Out of desperation I took my aunt's advice and started going to the Buddhist centre for satsang, but each time I had the same experience I've always had when I try to meditate: futile efforts to stop thinking, extreme physical discomfort, judgment of self and others, overwhelming drowsiness. Worse were the rare occa-sions when it "worked." When something "happened," and I felt the icy presence of the void, which it turns out is never more than a few seconds of thought-silence away.

The only thing left—the only thing that's ever been left when there's nothing else left—was books. I turned to the ones I read as a teenager with the same longing I felt back then. Drew tried to show an interest. I would read him something I loved from Krishnamurti or Pema Chodron or Thich Nhat Hanh, and he would look like he was listening, but when I asked what he thought he would say, "Sorry, babe, I have no idea what you're talking about."

Once I woke up in the middle of the night, stared at his pale, oval face, his wavy red hair and carefully trimmed beard, the freckles I used to find so adorable, and I felt protective of him, because he looked so wholesome and good, but at the same time I thought, *I would actually prefer to be dead than engaged to you.* It made no sense. He was lovely. And what was the alternative? Start over? It was too late.

One night, he woke me up from a nightmare. Or I woke him up. Apparently I was shouting.

"I need to go away," I said.

He groaned. "I just got promoted."

"I need to go by myself."

He said, "That's not a good idea" and fell back asleep as if he'd solved it.

I went to the living room and sat on the floor. I don't usually ask my aunt for advice, but I needed someone to tell me what to do, and if there's one thing Gina is good at, that's it. I checked the time difference. She was at home in New Zealand, where it was the next day and summer. She picked up after the third ring. I told her my woes. She talked about the Saturn return, how every twenty-nine years or so Saturn comes back to the position it was in at your birth, causing a life crisis, which is supposedly a good thing. I let her talk. Her voice was soothing.

"What should I do?" I asked. She's never liked Drew, neither of her adult children speak to her, and apart from her calamitous first marriage she's never had a long-term relationship, but I thought I could at least count on her to be prescriptive. Instead, she said, "Whatever the question, love is the answer."

"That's not an answer!" I said.

In the background I could hear the halting barks and beeps of tūī. "Pay attention," she said. "There are signs everywhere if you look for them. Go and sit somewhere quiet. Tune in to your higher self, and ask."

I don't know why, but when she said that, I felt the void gulping me into its orbit. It happened so quickly I had no chance to resist. It was horrendous.

"Oh, this is wonderful," she said. "I've chosen an angel card for you. Do you want to know what it is? It's Bliss!"

I hung up, picked myself up off the floor, found a candle and some matches, and went outside. There was a sheen of ice on the patio that cracked under my bare feet. I lit the candle, put it on the lid of the barbecue, looked up at the half moon and said, "I need a sign." What I really wanted was to get into bed with Drew and go back to sleep. I wanted so much to be comforted by him, but I knew that was over. I wished it wasn't, but it was.

I blew out the candle, went inside, and fell asleep on the couch. The next morning, I got my period for the first time in four months, and when I checked my emails, I had a message from one of the housesitting websites I'd registered for. It was June asking if I would be interested in housesitting her estate in South Bohemia. South Bohemia is where my mother was from, and I didn't apply for any housesits there. I wrote back immediately and said yes. Then I sat at my computer and wrote, *I want to wake up. I want to wake up. I want to wake up.*

Really, though, I wanted to disappear. Like my mother. Just vanish off the face of the earth.

IN ONE OF my earliest childhood memories, I was vomiting in a bucket in my bedroom while my mother and her only friend, an elderly Czech woman named Alžběta, howled with laughter in the living room.

When my father went away for work—or with his women, as I later learned—Teta Běta moved in. I hated it, because she bossed me around and forced me to eat disgusting foods, but on the other hand she took care of my mother, which meant I didn't have to.

I'd been learning about telepathy, and when I heard my mother laughing I closed my eyes and inwardly begged her to come to me. I knew she wouldn't hear if I called, because Teta Běta had shut the bedroom door. Even if she did get my message, she wouldn't have come. When she lived in London as a young refugee, she'd destroyed her back nursing "old fatties," as she called them, and it had made her reluctant to take care of anyone who was in less pain than her, which according to her was everyone.

That's not really fair. I'm told she was an attentive mother when I was little, but she stopped coping after we moved to Vancouver and especially after Teta Běta died. Unfortunately I don't remember anything before we moved to Vancouver, so the impression I'm left with is that she talked a lot about Czechoslovakia, complained a lot about her back, and hated most sounds. When she spoke about Czechoslovakia, she didn't mention family or·friends. She talked about the forests, the Vltava River, the Beskydy Mountains, the blossoming linden trees, and the music. Sometimes she played Czech songs all day long, and it made me hate those songs and the place they came from.

Years later, my father pointed out that my mother left us shortly after the Velvet Revolution, an event I imagined as some sort of glorious dress-up party. Having come up with so many stories to explain her disappearance to myself, I was told the real story was nothing more complicated than this: after twelve years in exile, she went home because she could.

I learned the truth when Gina and I met my father for their father's funeral. I was sixteen then and living with Gina in New Zealand, where I was in my last year of high school. My father had pushed for me to skip grades, in my mind so he could get rid of me sooner, but then he met Neary, and not long after that he sent me to finish school in New Zealand while he started his new life with her in Thailand.

I didn't mind. I was sick of being dragged along wherever he was filming, forced to go to schools for weeks or months at a time even when it made me feel like a freak show. And our relationship had been strained for a while. He'd given up on me during my mute phase. He told me I should get over myself, find a hobby, stop sulking in my bedroom listening to "that droner," as he called Leonard Cohen. I didn't blame him. I didn't blame anyone except myself and, later, my mother. Years after she left, I discovered that I hated her, and I was haunted by the idea that she allowed those boys on the bus to do what they did while I left my body and flew out the window.

We stayed with my great uncle's family, and after an awkward evening with relatives I'd never met, I was sent to share a bunk bed with a child I was told was my second cousin once removed.

"Your mummy's dead," she declared to the bottom of my bunk. I was half-asleep.

"What?"

"Your mummy is dead." I looked down at her. She had her feet in the air, and she was holding her toes and smiling.

My father said he was waiting to tell me in person after my grandfather's funeral. Gina said they didn't know themselves for a long time, because my mother had changed her next-of-kin. I accepted that. By then my mother's death was too abstract for mourning. I added the new information to my running autobiography—I was someone whose chronically-pained Czech mother disappeared and later overdosed on prescription opioids—and I didn't dwell on it except when other people's reactions to my apparent lack of feeling made me wonder if there was something wrong with me.

I was wondering that when I said goodbye to Drew at the airport. When it was time for me to go through security, he said "I won't give up on you. There's no line in the sand. Do whatever you have to do so you can come back and be happy with me." As I hugged him, the person who had been my best friend for years, I was calculating how long my money would last. My aunt had lent me enough to live on for a month, possibly two if I was careful. I had my credit card, and if I could manage to finish the new draft of my novel, I would get the second half of my puny advance. I'd also applied for a grant for something new, which was a long shot, but . . . *Jump and the net will appear,* Gina would say. *Be bold and trust.* Trust what? That the universe will support me to sip cappuccinos in Europe while other, apparently less bold and trusting people are forcibly displaced, trafficked, and wrongfully detained? That I will either transform into someone who sincerely cares about the things I wrote about in my grant application (finding one's roots, etc.) or find something else to write about that justifies consuming time and resources in a world on the brink? And *can* I even write? I don't know what I think about anything any more. I'm not sure I even know how to think. So how can I write if I can't think? Gina would say, *There's a higher way to see this.* And of course there is. Of course. But how can you sustain a higher way of seeing when working out what it even means to see, what we are even capable of seeing, is probably impossible, not because I'm a die-hard relativist, but because everything is too complex. I feel attacked by complexity, both amazed and disturbed by how certain other people seem to be.

I wouldn't admit it to anyone else, but after what happened in Sierra Leone, I can't totally dismiss my aunt's ideas about the universe. We all have our holy stories. I don't need to go on about mine, except to say that it happened while I was working for a medical NGO, and it involved an avalanche of synchronicities so absurd it was difficult not to entertain the possibility of some kind of destiny or guiding force, although even thinking that felt so wrong when I considered, for example, the brilliant young law student with schizophrenia who spent two years chained to a bed without access to diagnosis or treatment, or the blind twelve-year-old who came to a screening alone with rolled-up money tied by a piece of red yarn around her neck, who got all the way to the end of the process only to be told she needed a corneal transplant—in other words, she was too poor to see. A priest gave her the news. It was the saddest thing I've ever seen.

Part of my job was to write stories to be used for fundraising purposes. The stories were true, more or less, but obviously I didn't write every story. I didn't write about the girl with the red yarn, for example. That's nothing to do with the synchronicities, though. I can't talk about that without sounding like I'm trying to sell something, and I'm not.

Drew tucked my hair behind my ear. I'd been quiet for too long. He was going to read into it. I didn't want him to do that, but it would have been cruel to tell him I wasn't coming back, and apart from my guilt, which is my default anyway, I didn't feel at all conflicted about it.

He looked so miserable. "Let's be happy," I said. What I meant was, *please be happy without me.*

GINA OFFERED TO pay for me to visit her on my way to Europe. Although New Zealand is not on the way from Canada to the Czech Republic, I hadn't seen her in two years, and once I'd told Drew I wanted a temporary separation, I needed to be gone as quickly as possible. Normally I wouldn't have agreed to go to something called dance camp, which I gathered was some kind of international New Age peace gathering. For one thing, I don't dance in public. For another thing, although I'm mostly amused by and somewhat inured to my aunt's New Age stuff, I'd never actually participated in it. But she'd been looking forward to it all year, I didn't want her to miss out because of me, so I decided, as I have about so many things, that if it was awful, at least I could write about it. I did make one condition, though. She had to agree not to complain about anything—not the food, not the weather, not the organisation of the event, not people's body odour, nothing. She said she never complains, and I shouldn't be so judgmental.

She picked me up at the airport in Auckland, and after a couple of days with my father and his family, during which I nearly had a panic attack over a game of Hedbanz, she and I drove to Taranaki, stopping at hot pools and glowworm caves on the way. It was good to be with her, even though she spent a lot of time complaining about my father and embarrassing me with her unrelenting efforts to reform the world, or at least comment on it—lecturing waiters about tortured chickens, saying things like, "Look at that man's nose" when that man was well within earshot. She announced our arrival at the camp by honking her horn at a couple hugging in a field, even though there was plenty of space for her to drive around them.

I looked out the window at the tents and vans and beyond them some buildings and a big marquee. There were a lot more people than I had expected, which was a relief, because it meant I could go unnoticed.

We found a space in the campground, and Gina discovered she'd accidentally brought a single tent that would barely fit both of us and our sleeping bags. She parked her car next to the tent so we'd have somewhere to keep our things. While we were setting up, a man came and hugged her for a long time. She introduced us, and he hugged me, too.

"Most of the women wear skirts," he said, looking at my sweatpants.

"Is that right?" I said.

We heard someone calling haere mai, so we left our tent and walked toward the marquee. Everyone was gathering outside. A woman with white hair stood at the entrance calling us in, and someone called in response as we walked toward her.

As I stepped inside the marquee, the people on either side of me took my hands, and we walked to form a big circle. Someone was playing guitar, and everyone spontaneously sang something about being welcome in the family. When the circle reached back to the entrance, the first person did a U-turn, so we were passing each other face-to-face, singing to each other, making eye contact with one person after another.

When the music stopped, we made three concentric circles. In the middle of the inner circle was a bald man wearing purple pyjama bottoms and a T-shirt with *Plan Be* written on the front. He welcomed everyone, and they recited an opening prayer together. Then all of the circles took one step forward and some people said what I assume was the same prayer but in Māori. The circles stepped forward again, and the prayer was said in Spanish, French, German, Mandarin, and Arabic, with fewer people speaking each time.

"Namaste," the man said. "Let's say na-ma-ste."

People said it.

"Namaste. I bow to the place in you where the whole universe abides."

A woman went into the middle and stood next to him. "This dance is from the Hindu tradition," he said. "Repeat after me." The woman played guitar, and they both sang a pretty, slow melody with words in Sanskrit. The circle copied them.

"Follow the movements," he said. "Let's hold hands and start with the right foot." He held his arms out as if he was holding hands with neighbours on either side, and we sang together as we took four steps to the right, then released each other's hands and slowly turned counterclockwise, then held hands again and took two steps toward the centre while raising our arms, let go, pressed our hands together at our chests and bowed to the middle as we walked back two steps. When we'd repeated this sequence a few times, he said, "Only the outside circle now," and the two inner circles stopped singing. Then he called, "Now the middle circle," and my circle joined, creating a round. Then he told the inner circle to join, and the melody turned into beautiful harmonies.

It wasn't what I expected, but I liked the simplicity of the movements—I liked that there *were* movements—because not having to think about what to do with my body meant that I could relax somewhat.

For the next dance, there was a different leader. We had to make eye contact and turn in a circle with one person after another. The eye contact was a bit of a challenge. At first I was looking at the other people and wondering what they were

thinking, wondering if they were wondering what I was thinking, but after a while, and so gradually I didn't notice it was
happening, my mind stopped its ranging. I was doing the movements, repeating the words, looking into people's eyes, thinking,
thinking, thinking, and then the movements started happening
on their own, and I lost my sense of things.

My mind came back online when I saw that my aunt was
my next partner. It was unbearably intimate staring into her eyes,
and I could tell she was moved. I looked away.

There were more dances. A Sufi one, a Sikh one, a Christian
one. At the end, we huddled together in the middle with our arms
around each other and sang something about peace. We stayed in
silence apart from the odd sigh or moan until someone laughed,
and then everyone laughed. The huddle broke apart, and people
hugged each other. A stranger opened her arms to me. "You have
a strong Mary Magdalene energy," she said. I pulled away. "What
do you think of the dances?" she asked. "Is it too far out for you?"

"No," I said.

"It's just people coming together to dance and pray and celebrate, and that's a good thing!" she said.

I felt joy bubbling up in me, and I went back to the tent feeling calm for the first time in ages.

I WAS WOKEN in the night by Gina shaking our neighbour's tent
and shouting, "You're snoring!" When I woke up again, it was
morning, and she was gone. I pulled on some clothes. I was surprised to find that I was actually looking forward to going to the
marquee. Then I saw the note on Gina's windshield. It said, "Park
in the parking lot, like everyone else!"

Given the chance, I could have explained to the note's author
that there was barely enough room in our tent for our bodies,
the parking lot was a ten-minute walk away, and other people
had camper vans with awnings and outdoor *living rooms*, but I

couldn't explain any of that, because whoever wrote the note had done it anonymously.

I was so annoyed I would have read a book for the rest of the day if Gina hadn't showed up with coffee and proudly told me about the tent shaking, reminding me that we weren't exactly ideal camping companions after all.

Inside the marquee, people were walking and dancing around a drummer and a woman with a guitar. Gina took my hand, and I walked beside her and tried to see how many of the symbols on the walls I could identify. The cross, the Star of David, the nine-pointed star, the crescent and star, the yinyang, wheel, and om I knew. But the hand? The gate? The one with the swords?

When the music stopped, we made a circle, and the woman with the guitar said, "Kia ora, everyone."

"Are you here first time?" someone behind me whispered in a European accent.

I peered over my shoulder and saw the collar of a shirt.

"Yes," I said.

"Let's hold hands and close our eyes," the woman in the middle said.

The European took my hand, but the circle was so tight there was no space for him, so I reached over my shoulder, and both of our hands rested there.

A man read a verse from a Persian poet. "The people of this world are like the three butterflies in front of a candle's flame. The first one went closer and said, *I know about love.* The second one touched the flame lightly with his wings and said, *I know how love's fire can burn.* The third one threw himself into the heart of the flame and was consumed. He alone knows what true love is."

"But I know you," the European whispered. "You had to be on some other dances."

I looked back. Curly black hair, plaid shirt, bare chest, pounamu. I turned away, using a toddler's logic—*if I can't see him, he can't see me.* "I don't think so," I said.

"But I definitely met you before," he whispered. "So if it was not here it had to be on some other dances."

"I don't think so," I said.

The woman in the middle told us to choose partners and make two circles, one facing in and one facing out. The European faced me from the inner circle. He held my hands, and I looked past him to watch the leader demonstrate the dance. I thought he would turn around and watch her too, but he kept staring at me. I tried to look at him again. I caught a quick glimpse of his eyes before I had to look away.

LATER THAT DAY, Gina and I were having lunch under a tree when he found me. "I remembered how I know you," he said. "Were you on New Zealand two years ago?"

I told him I was.

"And were you on one retreat centre nearby Taupō?"

I looked at him properly. It was much worse than I'd thought. He was like a more elegant version of one of those bodice ripper men. Green eyes, full lips, hairless, muscular chest.

"I think so," I said. "Just for five minutes. We stopped to return a book." I felt salad dressing dripping onto my thumb. I put my plate down and wiped my hand on the grass. When I looked at him again, he seemed to be full of emotion.

"I met you," he said.

"Really?"

"Actually, I didn't. I saw you. On the hallway."

"How can you remember that two years later?" someone interjected, and I realised the people around us were listening.

"How can you forget that?" He gestured toward my face. I couldn't believe he hadn't noticed how gross my skin was.

I held out my hand. "I'm Mája," I said.

"Kuba." He took my hand in his big, smooth palm. "Are you from New Zealand?"

For the sake of simplicity I said yes, assuming he wouldn't pick up on my accent.

"I love New Zealand," he said. "It's the only place I can imagine to live, apart from my homeland."

I'd never heard anyone use that word in normal conversation before. "Where's that?" I asked.

"Czech Republic," he said. I kept holding his hand, watching his mouth. "Small country in the middle of Europe."

IT TOOK FOUR days for June and Pieter to leave, and now that they're gone, I've realised I don't want to be alone after all—at least not in a decaying mansion with a potential rapist for a neighbour.

Kuba is in India visiting his sitar teacher. I've only been able to Skype with him once since I've been here, but it's like an addiction—I think about him all the time, which is nuts, because I don't know him at all.

When we speak, he's as intense as he was at camp. "It's not so easy," he says one night. "Once upon a time I met women who told me they want to be with me only for one time, no commitment, but they always end up crying. But now I am the one saying, *No! Forever!*"

At dance camp, I avoided him after he told me he remembered me from two years earlier. His beauty and confidence made me uncomfortable, and I had no interest in getting involved with him or anyone else so soon after leaving Drew. I wouldn't even have told him I was going to the Czech Republic if Gina hadn't jumped into our conversation when he said where he was from.

That afternoon she had a headache and went to lie down. I went to a workshop where I was supposed to find out about my past lives, but when I told the facilitator I'm a writer he recounted every detail of his sci-fi novel. I went to a couple of the dances, but I didn't see Kuba. I swam in the river, skipped stones with kids, had some normal conversations and a couple of quite odd ones.

After my swim, I was approached by a middle-aged man I'd never seen before. "I wanted to say thank you for coming here," he said. "It was wonderful to meet your energy. When are you leaving?"

"In the morning," I said.

He asked if he could hug me, and I let him even though I found him gross. "I'd love to do something for you before you go," he said. "Can I give you a shoulder rub?"

"Maybe later," I said, then someone blew the conch, so I had an excuse to escape.

After dinner, I went to the marquee. Kuba was in the middle talking to two women who were both standing very close to him. He was holding a guitar, so I guessed he must be playing music for the dances. It was all somehow unsettling, and I decided I would not speak to him again.

Someone tapped my arm. "How about that shoulder rub?"

In certain situations, it's like my will is disabled. It was much worse when I was a teenager, before I became—or seemed to become—self-possessed in a way that discourages people from taking liberties.

I expected him to lead me to the "snuggle pit," a pile of pillows set up in an annex built into the side of the marquee, but instead he went outside, and I followed him. He led me to a tent where he had a massage table set up. "Take off everything except your knickers and lie down here," he said. I couldn't think of one thing to say to get out of it. Before he left, he said, "You can take off your knickers too, if you want."

I removed my T-shirt and sweatpants and lay face-down on the table. I heard him rubbing oil into his hands, and as he oiled up my bare skin, I made an inventory of all the other times in my life I've endured men doing things to me that I didn't want them to do because what? I thought I'd invited it somehow? It would be too embarrassing to say no? I didn't want to hurt their feelings?

"I'm going to undo this," he said. He unhooked the clasp of my bra and moved the straps to the side.

When he got to my underwear, he said, "Can I pull these down?"

"Um, prefer not," I squeaked.

He moved his hands up to my shoulders then down my back. When he got to my underwear again, he said, "I'm going to move these out of the way," and he slipped them down and started to massage my bare bum. At that point, saying nothing became harder than saying no.

"My aunt is sick," I said, keeping my face in the hole at the end of the massage table. "I have to check on her."

"Do you want me to . . ."

"No. Thank you."

"I'll be outside," he said.

When I came out, he was saying something, but I ignored him and ran away barefoot over the sharp gravel.

I didn't want to lie awake scolding myself all night, so I had a shower, reapplied my makeup in a bathroom stall, and went back to the marquee. The dances had finished, and Kuba was in the middle hugging a woman. His chin rested on top of her head, and she stood on the balls of her feet with her ear to his chest.

When he pulled away from her, another woman reached out to him, and I realised there was a queue of people waiting to hug him. While he was hugging the next person, he looked up and our eyes met. He let the person he was hugging go and came to me. Neither of us spoke. He put his arms around me and rested his cheek on my head. I clasped my hands behind his back and listened to his heartbeat.

We agreed to meet in the dining room in ten minutes. I spent half an hour waiting for him, drinking tea and listening to a woman who had been through a nasty divorce. She told me the past life workshop leader had shown up naked in her tent the night before, and she'd briefly wondered if that was the best she could do now before coming to her senses and telling him to get out. She was doing a hilarious impression of him, but when Kuba appeared, she changed.

"What's in the bag?" she asked. She touched his arm.

He looked at me. "Are you ready for chat?"

I said goodnight to the woman and followed him outside to the porch, where he'd prepared a pot of tea and two cups. It was easier to look at him in the moonlight. We were facing each other cross-legged on a couch, and our knees almost touched.

We drank tea and talked about India. He was going there the following week. He asked what I do, and when I told him I'm a writer, he said, "It's wonderful."

I asked what he does.

"I have a van which is full of music instruments," he said. "And I drive around and play with people." I assumed that meant he was unemployed.

"What kind of music do you play?" I asked.

"Mostly music for dances and Czech folk songs, which are very special thing," he said.

I thought of the songs my mother played when I was a child, the ones I hated, probably because they made me feel like she would prefer to be somewhere else, which turned out to be true. Now I was curious to know what they meant, to him and to Czechs in general, but I didn't want to lapse into interview mode. One more question, and then I would let him ask me something.

"What's special about them?" I asked.

"It's different in different parts," he said. "Because there's unique feeling in Šumava, which is different from feeling in

Krkonoše or Beskydy or Bílé karpaty. And there are even micro-regions, like in South Moravia, for example, there is a very specific region which includes just few villages, and next region includes next villages, and they have different patterns in the music, different melodies, and often different rhythm and way of using instruments, and it feels natural that it responds to the energies which are present in that landscape."

I was listening, but I was also imagining what it would be like to have sex with him. I guessed I would feel like I was corrupting him, because he seemed so pure. "Is that different from other folk music?" I asked, breaking my one question rule.

"Yes and no," he said. "I think the music is the language of Czech people. It's like it's proved by history, it's shaped so long. It's really stroking me."

I told him my mother was Czech, and he looked shocked. When he asked where she was from, I said Prague because I didn't want to try and pronounce České Budějovice, and I assumed I would never see him again.

"And where does she live now?" he asked.

"She died," I said. I usually say passed away, but I wasn't sure if he would understand.

He didn't look embarrassed or make a sympathetic face or try to touch me. "So do you have some family members in Czech?"

"I don't know," I said. "My mother wasn't in contact with her family."

"Do you know what was her surname?"

"Svobodová."

"So you probably have few thousands of family members there."

He asked if I like the dances, and I told him the truth: I have a hard time getting out of my head.

"Wait," he said. "If your mum is from Czech, does it mean you are Mája with the j?"

"Yes."

"So are you Marie?"

"Yes."

"Wow," he said.

"What?"

"Just wow!" he said. "Májenka."

"My mother called me Májuška sometimes," I said.

"Can I hug you, Májuška?" he asked.

I nodded, and he moved closer and put his arms around my waist. We were ear to ear. He was shaking. I couldn't believe he was attracted to me. I knew the evidence was strong, but it seemed impossible. Not that I'm not used to being desired by men—just not men like him, if there is such a thing.

Our mouths found each other. I wanted to feel all of it, but I couldn't. I was thinking too much, and he was still shaking.

"Are you okay?" I said.

He sat back and looked at me.

"What about your name?" I asked.

"What about it?"

"Czechs have like ten versions of their names, right? What are yours?"

"Well, I am Jakub."

"Yes?"

"And mostly people call me Kuba."

"What should I call you?"

"Kubíku. Or if you want me to do something, Kubíčku. Or we can go further. Jakoubku, Jakoubek. If the something you want me to do is very hard you can try Jakoubečku."

He picked up his guitar and tuned it, then he sang a song in Czech. I watched the fingers of his left hand on the frets, the finger and thumb of his right hand deftly plucking the strings.

"What's it about?" I asked.

"It's from Vlasta Redl," he said. "It shows about how our whole world is just small thing. Because here is Zlín, a little town in Czech, and then around the corner there's Melbourne, there's San Francisco, and you can relax, and here's your drink. I will be back shortly."

"I love your voice," I said.

"I would like to take a sleeping bag and mattress and show you one nice place," he said.

I tried to remember what underwear I had on, which reminded me of that other man's hands on my body. "My aunt will be worried," I said.

"Write for her *Don't be afraid* and put it on the pillow."

"That would really freak her out."

"What?"

"Okay," I said.

While I waited for Kuba to come back, I imagined Drew digging out his car, defrosting his windshield, driving to work in the sleet, coming home in the dark.

"Come, beloved one." Kuba held out his hand, and for the second time that night I found myself following a strange man into the darkness, feeling like I was in a story someone else was making up, only this time I couldn't wait to find out what happened next.

He led me to a tree in a meadow. He set up the mattress and sleeping bag, and we lay down together. He was shaking again.

"You're freezing!" I said. He looked so young.

"It is not from cold that I am shaking," he said. He touched my cheek. "You are full of beauty."

When we kissed, I thought of Drew again. It was like a cruel joke. The girl who broke your heart is making out with another man, and it's *this* guy.

"I have a fiancé," I said. "Sort of."

He stopped kissing me. "What means fiancé?" he asked.

"It's when you promise to get married. But I don't want to be married to him. I don't want to be married to anyone, actually. So I left."

"When?"

"Last week."

"Don't you think you are bit crazy woman?"

"Do you?"

"Yes, I think I am a bit crazy woman sometimes," he said. "When I saw you two years ago, I was here on New Zealand with my ex-partner, Liliana, and I was also feeling the same what you are describing. I was not happy, not wanting to continue the partnership but afraid to end it. When I saw you on the hall, I felt like, if I have this person next to me, I can do anything. I can change the whole world. So it's the reason why it was so strong, and why I can remember two years later. When I look at you, I am filled with inspiration."

"How old are you?" I asked.

"Twenty-eight."

"So you're next," I said. I expected him to ask what I meant, and I was going to tell him about the Saturn return, but instead he pulled me closer and said, "In Czech, we say the silence is golden."

It confirmed what I already knew. I said, "Mlčeti zlato," and if he was surprised, he didn't let on, maybe for the same reason.

HE CRIED WHEN we said goodbye. He was staring at me again, and I was thinking about my skin. He took my hand and held it to his chest. "I wanted to tell you that it is very hard for me," he said. "I am not use to allow my heart to go to something only for now."

I was going to ask him if he could imagine us meeting by chance in another two years. I said, "Can you imagine . . ."

"Yes!" he interrupted me.

"Okay, what can you imagine?"

"I can imagine living with you. I can imagine you the mother of my children. I can imagine us in a small house, close to the nature. Can I have your contact?"

I laughed. It was hard to believe he existed in reality, but I gave him my email address and Gina's number.

He kissed my forehead, then he hugged me, and when I pulled back he opened my hand and pressed something into my palm.

"Let me know if you're going to be in Wellington," I said. I started to walk away.

"Beloved one!" he called. I wondered if he'd forgotten my name. He held up his phone. "Can I make a photo? For the contacts?"

I let him take my picture, and as I walked toward the campground, I opened my palm and saw two conjoined crystals. I found it corny, but also sweet.

Gina was watching me from across the field. "You look lovely together," she said when I was close enough to hear, and to my amazement she left it at that.

AFTER THE CAMP, I was in a strange state. I can't describe it, except to say that in the very best way nothing mattered, and I was content to sit on Gina's balcony in silence all day. When she tried to interact with me, I found I didn't have much to say. It wasn't that I didn't want her around, but just being together was enough.

Kuba didn't write, but I didn't mind. I saw our meeting as a sign I was on the right path, and I didn't need anything more from him. Then two days before my flight to Prague, he sent an email asking why I hadn't answered him. It turned out he'd been sending texts to Gina's landline. He wrote, "I am singing for you every day. I sent your picture to my mother, and she was so touched, because she was dreaming something big is happening for me."

I wrote back immediately, but it was too late—I was leaving for Europe, and he was leaving for India. There was no time left. And I'd lost the crystals he gave me. I searched for them everywhere.

I convinced myself it was for the best. I couldn't afford to be distracted by a charismatic musician who has women lining up to hug him. I needed to be alone and to write. I need to. But since Pieter and June left, I've succeeded only in being alone. I was counting on a moody, inspiring kind of aloneness, but this kind—the dirty house, the guilt, the fear of never having a family or a normal life—is not healthy. And I miss writing so much. I miss my writer self, Maya. She's much cleverer and braver than I am, and she would love this place.

During the day I cook, eat, read, take Sarie for runs, and check if Kuba is on Skype, the compulsiveness of my checking proof that I should stick to my decision not to visit him in Prague. I've reread our last messages so many times. The day I flew to Czech, he wrote,

> My beloved jewel Mája, thank you for the amazing time we spent together. What I feel is a fresh flame in my heart if I think about you. And I want to ask: Will you consider to come and stay with me when you are finished with the housesitting? Please say yes and I will prepare all!
>
> Kisses from Delhi,
> Jakub

In response, I wrote:

> Kubíku,
>
> Thank you for the kind offer. I would love to visit you sometime, but not right now. I hope you will understand. I can't go from one relationship into another one. Enjoy India!
>
> Mája

It makes sense that he wouldn't respond to that. My answer was clear. I'm focusing on other things. I'm trying to.

The something-is-coming dreams are constant. Mostly I'm locking doors and windows or being forced into horrific sexual situations. And I'm getting weird. Middle school weird. It takes me all morning to psych myself up to go grocery shopping. I can't remember what June said about whether Tesco, Lidl, or Penny Market is best, so I go to Penny Market because it sounds cheap. I end up spending over an hour wandering around looking at people's faces, the pink meat, the reams of brown baked goods. As I'm laying my purchases on the belt at the cash register I realise I've chosen all the wrong things, but I can't take them back, because I want to appear to know what I'm doing. The lady says something without looking up from the scanner. I smile and say ne. She doesn't smile back.

When I get home, Kuba has finally written:

Beloved Mája. To be honest, we don't know each other. We were one night together and it was amazing. But we can't plan a lot about the future. Dreams and intentions, but we will see what will come after we meet. Don't be afraid, all options are the best. Don't define the status of our relationship too early. Let's flow and feel. Today I had amazing walk in mountains, so it helped me to be more peaceful—trees, snow peaks, praying flags, monasteries . . .

Don't define the status of our relationship too early? What does that mean? And what does he mean, *all options are the best?* And *after we meet?* I told him I wasn't going to visit him. I need to speak to him immediately, but he's hardly ever on Skype.

I'M JOGGING WITH Sarie, listening to the *Ram Dass Here and Now* podcast on my iPod. I call Ram Dass my Ram Dad, because he gives the best advice, and I've heard all his jokes and stories a hundred times. Now he's talking about how you have to become somebody before you can start to become nobody.

I wonder if that's why I'm here—to find out who I am so I can get over myself.

Today is the seventh anniversary of my first date with Drew. Last year, we celebrated with a trip to Montréal. We stayed at the Sheraton, saw Cirque du Soleil and Hey Rosetta! and ate at Crudessence and Aux Vivres. This year I woke up to a puddle of dog pee in the kitchen, ate my last protein bar for breakfast, and opened my emails to find a message from my publisher terminating my contract. They didn't mention the advance.

A tractor pulls up next to me. Behind the wheel is a grey-skinned man with a thin, patchy beard and several missing teeth. He's speaking. I take out my ear buds. He says something in Czech. I say, "Sorry, I don't understand."

"Who you are?" he says.

"I'm Mája."

"Where from?"

"New Zealand."

"Pieter?" he says.

"Back tomorrow," I lie.

"Where sleep you?" he says. Surely I've misheard him. I cup my hand to my ear. "Zimmer," he says.

"Sorry, I don't understand." I look back toward the house. "I have to go," I say. I smile. Like in my nightmares, I'm employing the brilliant tactic of trying to appease a potential attacker by being cute.

I'm coming down the road to the gate when he steps out of the woods. How did he get there? He's a few hundred metres in front of me, watching me run toward him. I want to shout, *You are so creepy, go away!* Instead, when I'm close enough for him to hear me, I smile and say, "Ahoj."

"Tractor," he says, pointing the wrench he's holding toward the forest.

"Yes?"

"We go," he says.

"I have an appointment, sorry." I wave at him and continue to jog, and when I turn back, he's still watching me.

At the house I lock and bolt all of the doors. I'm too scared to go outside to feed the birds. Sometimes I truly hate being a woman. I call Pieter and June and tell them what happened. They think it's hilarious. After they hang up, I try to find someone to chat to, but no one's online, so I distract myself by checking Kuba's Facebook. He has about 3,000 friends, and everything he posts gets at least 100 likes. A woman named Pavla has tagged him in hundreds of photos. It looks like they were in a band together. There's one photo where they're staring into each other's eyes on a candlelit stage with a circle of people around them watching.

A Facebook chat pops up. It's Drew. *Happy anniversary, sweetie. What's your address over there?* I know I have to tell him it's over, but I don't think he's stable enough to take it yet. His best friend wrote me, "Drew's having a nervous breakdown, but I hope you're having fun eating, praying, and loving." I wrote back, *Fuck you*, but I didn't hit send.

Before I can talk myself out of it, I write, *Are you there?*

He must have lost ten pounds. I wasn't prepared for that. He says, "I had breakfast with Becca today. We toasted you with our green smoothies."

"I need to tell you something," I say.

He lowers his head like he's waiting for me to drop a guillotine. I tell him. He puts his hands over his face. I wait. He asks if there's anything he could have done differently. I say no. He asks if there's anything he can do or say to change my mind. I say no.

He starts to cry.

"Look, it's late here."

"Come on, it's *us*," he says. "You can't do this!"

I want to close the computer and sleep, but my guilt stops me. More than anything, I feel guilty for my lack of feelings, and once again I wonder if I'm missing some necessary parts. Looking at myself in the Skype window while Drew is choking back his tears, I think, *I should put on concealer in case Kuba comes online.*

When it's over, I Skype with Becca. I thank her for taking care of Drew and forward her Kuba's email. "What the hell?" she says. "Don't define the status of your relationship too early? He told you he wanted to have babies with you after knowing you for less than twenty-four hours."

"I know, I know."

"Listen, you don't want to hear this, but do you really think you have anything in common with this person? I mean, *Let's flow and feel?*"

"I can't explain it. You'd have to meet him."

"So he can hypnotise me too? No thanks. Look, I support you, and I'm sure you know what's best for you, but be careful, okay?"

I tell her about the farmer. "Can you come here?" I ask.

"You want me to bring the kids?"

"Forgot about them."

"I'm reading *Testament of Youth*," she says, "and there's this poem by Rupert Brooke about how the safest thing of all is death."

"This is your pep talk?"

"Well, someone could attack you and kill you and then you'd be dead. So what?"

"Uh huh."

"Okay, you might not find that as helpful as I do."

It seems impossible for the farmer to break in and rape me while I'm Skyping with Becca, but after I hang up, my situation seems even more dire than before. I take Sarie to the bedroom where I slept when June and Pieter were here. She seems scared, too. She crawls under the blanket with me and whines. I look out the window at the moon, which is full. I can hear the wind outside and Sarie's breathing.

I say, "I need another sign. If it's real, please, one more."
I open my computer and write to Kuba.

> I know we can't make any plans, and I have no expectations.
> Let's meet and see what happens. I'll come to Prague if you
> still want me to. When are you back?

I hit send before I can change my mind, then reread. What a load
of bullshit. I knew all along I was going to visit him. Of course I
am. I have nothing else to do, and he's the most magnetic person
I've ever met. And of course I have expectations. Everyone has
expectations.

The dog is whining again. I close my eyes and mentally
scan my body. I picture a lighthouse and a tranquil sea. I picture
Kuba's face, his eyes, his hands, his chest, his back . . .

When I open my eyes, he's already responded.

> My Love, amazing, you will come! It looks like perfect plan.
> I will organise the train for you. I am hoping if my place
> will be okay for you, because it is basic, and there is my
> wild friend.
>
> I arrived Czech Republic yesterday. It's nice, but I am still
> a little bit in another world. Some mouse was in here once
> upon a time, so it is hard to clean and wash and fix . . . I will
> be very busy with the music and other work soon and I am
> so much looking forward. We organise a ceremony with
> the Siberian shamans in the local forest starting very soon,
> and tomorrow I am also very busy. I will try to write you
> more on Saturday, or we can Skype. Sunday morning?
>
> Miss you, thank you for beauty what you bring to my life.
> Hug hug hug hug hug

I run to the bathroom to look in the mirror, but when I get back
and try to find him on Skype, he's gone. It's Friday, and now I
have to wait until Sunday. I wish I could sleep until then.

I write to tell him I'll buy my own train ticket and ask what he means by "wild friend." I tell him not to worry about his place too much. I've lived in much more basic situations I'm sure, and I'm looking into renting a short-term apartment until I decide what to do next.

I SPEND SATURDAY looking for apartments in Prague and wishing it was Sunday. Kuba doesn't contact me again until Tuesday, though, but when he apologises and tells me how busy he's been preparing for my visit, I pretend not to know we had a plan at all.

I tell him about Drew. His parents have removed me from Facebook. I guess when they said they loved me like a daughter they meant they would love me as long as I was filling that role.

Kuba tells me about Pavla, the woman who posted all the photos of him. They were in a punk band when he was in his teens, then they were in a folk ensemble, and then they had success as a duo called Vesmír, playing spiritual and meditation music they cowrote.

He says he was afraid people would be angry with him when he split up their band, but he was amazed by how much support he got. "Even her father," he says. "He said he wishes his daughter to be happy, but did I notice how she is?"

"How is she?"

"He was sure she was supposed to have medication, because it was impossible to understand her."

"Did you understand her?"

"It was quite mission," he says.

"What did you like about her?"

"I appreciate how she is spontaneous, and she has excitement. She is definitely not grey colour person, and she always say whatever she feels, good or bad, so some people don't like it, but I like it."

I close Skype and check my messages. I have a missed call from Drew and a single email:

Please don't do this.

I don't even know what I'm doing. Until I turned thirty, I thought thirty was the age when people became adults. It's probably not a coincidence that it's also the age my mother was when she left. Now I'm thirty, and not only am I not an adult, I'm not sure I even know anyone who is. I guess Becca has hit all the grown-up milestones, but she's miserable.

I create a document and begin:

What I know: If there's something guiding me, I don't have to follow. But if it's real, it led me to Kuba. And the question isn't if I'm going to marry him and have babies with him. It's right now, is he the key to something I urgently need to find out? I believe the answer is yes.

I turn out the light, pull the blankets up to my nose, and whisper to myself, "Yes, yes, yes."

THANKS TO THE farmer, I'm too afraid to go jogging or out of the house at all, except to feed the birds, which I do quickly and always with Sarie. She's stopped eating. I guess it's her way of protesting against the lack of exercise. I miss our jogs, too. They were the only thing that helped me to feel calm.

Every time I fall asleep, I have nightmares. Last night, I dreamt the farmer was standing at the end of my bed. His tractor was in the garden, and the light was blazing in the window. He crawled onto me and pressed his thumbs into my ribs. It hurt so much, but I couldn't move or shout. Without opening his mouth, he said, "Don't be afraid." When I woke up, the walls were shaking, and my ribs hurt.

Kuba's communication is detached and unhelpful. He writes things like, *Let's observe it* in response to urgent practical questions. I asked if he could tell me if the apartments I like are in good areas, and instead of answering, he sent me his schedule, which is alarmingly full and makes no sense. One whole day says *FROG*. He wrote:

> Please write me as soon as possible what you would like to join. I have to plan a lot.

I DREAMT THAT I was in a room with an open window. I was wearing bloody underwear, and there was hair everywhere. I knew a giant gorilla had been in there, and he'd raped me, and he was coming back. He had a GPS implanted in my body. I got in a cab and went to the hospital, but the gorilla was there like King Kong, picking up the cabs and checking inside, looking for me.

Pieter and June decided to come home early after I told them Sarie isn't eating. The day before they arrive I finally get a proper email from Kuba. He asks if we can talk about the apartments when I'm there. One of them is already taken, and the guy who owns the other one is getting fed up with waiting, so it will probably be taken by then, too, but it's too late to do anything about it. Kuba writes:

> I had very wild day today. Tonight I will do workshops in Moravia. In the evening tomorrow I will need to be on internet, because of two hundred e-mails waiting for me, so we can chat or call, but it will be about 9 p.m. Can you be on-line for a while? And can we plan a bit what you will join here? It is so many things to do. My head is very tired, my body the same. It is hard. I planned it, but it is hard. Yesterday at full-moon night we did dances around the fire on the hill in the middle of Prague. It was perfect. Nature, fire, circle, and city lights background. It is so good to be with open people. I will be there to pick you at the station. It will be a bloody meeting. I will eat you!

WHEN PIETER AND June arrive, Pieter cooks steak for Sarie, but she won't touch it. June cries and Pieter hugs her. They don't talk to me much.

I take my computer to the bedroom and check if Kuba is on Skype. He isn't, but there's an email from him.

> My beloved, I had long, hard, but amazing day. Big healing through music and sacred steps. And many new drums came to the world. It is so hard to wait for opportunity to touch you.

He signs off *Have a nice dreams, I hope I am in them.* He wouldn't say that if he knew about my dreams.

I take off all of my clothes and examine myself in the bathroom mirror. I'm too thin. I have stretch marks on my thighs from losing weight too quickly. I shine the light directly onto my face. My skin is uneven and blotchy close up. My scars look redder in the harsh light. I have bags under my eyes. I back up. I want to see how far from the mirror I have to be to look pretty, but the bathroom isn't big enough.

Finally Kuba comes online. I say my camera isn't working because I don't want him to see me. He asks if I've had a chance to look at his schedule, so I bring it up on my screen. One weekend says LIÁNA. He says it means ayahuasca. An Amazonian curandero will be guiding a ceremony in the summer.

When Drew and I went to Peru for his fieldwork, it seemed like every tourist we met was talking about ayahuasca. I was intrigued by the idea of a plant helping people to sort themselves out, but I was too scared to try it myself, especially after reading about women being abused and people having psychotic episodes or seizures or being left alone in the jungle to die.

"Would you like to join it?" he says. I have no idea if I'll even be in Europe then.

"Can I share something with you?" I ask.

"Of course."

"So, recently I went through this period when a lot of synchronicities happened to me. Do you know what synchronicities are?"

He laughs. "Since I met you I don't experience anything else than synchronicities."

"Okay, so I'm a skeptical person, but this was so extreme that eventually I couldn't ignore it, so I decided that from then on I was going to say yes to everything."

"And what happened?"

"It was terrifying. And it changed my life. I think it's still changing my life."

He says, "I relate it to the initiation. Because by taking the action towards the darkness you are proving you trust, not just by words, but by the action you face the unknown and do it consciously, believing you are protected somehow. When I slept alone in the forest first time I was scared by every sound, every shape, but I did it because I trust I am held. Or when I flew to South America without even knowing buenos días . . . It's like self-initiation, isn't it?"

"I guess so," I say. "But what about people who trust and something terrible happens?"

"I don't know," he says. "I only know what's true for myself. So will you join me for the ayahuasca?"

I say yes, and like when I was in Sierra Leone, I don't fully trust, but I also don't feel any doubt.

"Speaking about the synchronicities," he says. "I found a home for us."

"Where's that?"

"One place we can live in a bus I'm planning to buy. There were so many signs I'm supposed to connect with a place and live there with you, and I was drawing it with things I would like to build there like a yurt and sauna. And then unbeliev-able circumstances happened! I went to visit our friend who lives in the cottage in the nature, and she was saying some-times there are the owls doing circles above that place, which is very rare. There are people who never saw owl in their life in Czech Republic. Then she was saying you can live there on that hill with your Mája if you like, and I drove up the hill and see it's totally as I was drawing it in my pictures, including the out-house, sauna, yurt, the shape of the forest behind. I was running all around the top of the hill and singing and saying, *I found the home for me and Mája.* And then on my way back to Prague, I was seeing many times three repeating numbers on the license plates, which is the sign that I'm on the good way, and then I found owl on the road, which was really unbelievable, and I saw it as welcoming home."

"Was the owl dead?"

He laughs. "Of course."

I assume his story is meant to affirm what I said, but it's having the opposite effect, because if his vision is real, I can't see myself in it. What I really want to know is if he has other lovers and why, of all people, he wants to live with me. I'd like to show him what I really look like or see myself how he seems to see me. But I have to be careful. Until now, none of this has been real, but it's about to get very real, and I have to be ready.

I'VE PICTURED THIS moment so many times: my outfit—a dress, for him—how I would step out of the train and time would stop as we looked at each other, how he would kiss me, everything perfect. But that was in the past, when there was time for my scars to fade, for my clothes to look right, for me to become detached and confident and ready. None of those things have hap-pened. As usual, despite my plans, I'm still imperfect, insecure, and wearing pants.

I don't see him on the platform. I can't look around too much, because I don't want to appear pathetic, so I drag my suitcase out of the way and stand in front of a huge poster with bold white text and a date over what looks like lizard scales. When Kuba finally appears, I wonder if he hung back on purpose, because he wanted a chance to decide if he was going to do this, whatever this is.

He puts his hands on my shoulders. He is literally stunning, like Tennyson's Lancelot with his "coal-black curls." His shirt says *In Reality, It's a Game.* There's a Nokia logo on the sleeve. As usual, my brain is ruining everything. When he brushes my hair away from my face to kiss me, all I can think about is how my skin looks in the sunlight.

His van is full of chimes, feathers, stones, and symbols that jingle and clang as we drive. I imagine he expects me to be dazzled by Prague, but I've seen it before, and there's only so much beauty a person can take in. I was worried it would be awkward, and we would have nothing to talk about, but he talks the whole time. He keeps interrupting himself to show me license plates with three repeating numbers, and I wonder: is he not very intelligent and I don't notice because of the language thing, or is he much more sophisticated than I realise?

The license plates remind me of his story about the dead owl. I ask him what he did with it.

"I still have her," he says.

"Where?"

"She is nearby."

"Where?"

He looks over his shoulder. "Don't be afraid," he says. "She doesn't stink."

He tells me his "wild friend," Otto, wanted their house to be a centre for Buddhism and ecological activism, but he has a hard time getting along with people, so he spends his time protecting the local forest by doing daily patrols where he picks up garbage and sets up barriers against 4-wheelers.

"He is lovely man who is very bitter," Kuba says. "And he experienced a very hard life, and he doesn't trust people, and he hates women." He stops outside of a gate and pulls on the emergency brake. "Welcome home!"

It's clear that the house is the odd one out on their narrow suburban street. All of the others are tidy, with lacy white curtains and planter boxes in the windowsills, but this one is shrouded by creepers and draping electrical wires, and the concrete fencepost is decorated with handprints like the ones in Paleolithic caves. The garden is overgrown, and dotted amid the long grass are crystals and Buddhas and metal statues of something that looks like an alien with spears through its body.

We climb a rusty metal stairway and enter the house upstairs. Inside, there's another small stairway leading to a landing where there's a fridge, a rain-damaged piano under a skylight, and a bathroom that isn't actually a room, because instead of a door there's a purple and white-chequered curtain.

Off the landing, there are two doors. While Kuba is unlocking one, the other opens, and a scruffy middle-aged man comes out. He says something in German and offers me his hand. I shake it, and he disappears into his room and returns with a plate on which there is a cube of bread and a mound of salt. "Czechish tradition," he says. He speaks to Kuba in Czech. There's a healthy-looking mouse eating something from a plate on the stove behind him.

"Salt is life, and bread is life," Otto says in slow English, holding the plate toward me. I tear a small piece off the cube of bread, dip it in the salt, and bypass my gluten anxiety to put it in my mouth. I'm touched by his gesture, but I don't think it would be a good idea to hug him if he hates women.

KUBA'S ROOM, WHICH he calls our room, is cluttered but clean and charming. There's a woodstove, a kitchenette, a desk, a low table with cushions around it, and a loft bed. The walls are covered in pictures, symbols, stickers, flags, and wings, and there are musical instruments everywhere. Next to the table is a shrine with rocks, feathers, pieces of wood, photographs, religious trinkets, and one of those alien figures with the spears through it.

Kuba drops my suitcase, and we undress and climb the ladder to the bed. I can't describe what happens between us without desecrating it somehow, except to say that, possibly for the first time in my life, I'm certain I'm exactly where I'm meant to be.

Afterwards, we lie with our limbs entwined. I tell him I saw a mouse in Otto's room. I wouldn't have said anything if it had been on the floor, but the way it was casually dining on the stove was worrisome.

"Don't be afraid," he says. "In here are no mice."

We have a shower, and I'm careful not to get water on my face. There's a miniature ladder in the basin with a tiny sign at the top.

"Otto made that after the mouse was trapped there," Kuba says.

"What does it say?"

"There is written *Become a Buddha*."

WHEN I WAS a teenager, there was a period when everywhere I went I saw a man with white-blonde hair and blue eyes. I'd never seen him before, then suddenly I saw him everywhere.

One day, he passed me and Gina on the sidewalk. It was raining. I saw him coming and wanted to smile at him, but when he got close, I covered my face with my umbrella.

"Did you know that person?" Gina asked.

"No. Why?"

"He gave you the loveliest smile."

I promised myself that I'd talk to him the next time I saw him, but I never saw him again. Now I wonder if that experience prepared me for Kuba—this feeling that I have to hold on to every moment, because nothing like this will ever happen to me again.

For days, we don't leave the house except to go to the supermarket and for walks in the forest. In the mornings, I get up before him and sneak into the bathroom to put on concealer. When he wakes up, we sit in front of his altar together. He lights a candle, sometimes he drums or prays or plays a Tibetan singing bowl. Then he meditates, and I watch him and think.

Those figures Otto has everywhere—Kuba has one on his altar—are renderings of the "wounded man" painted in Pech Merle cave in France. There's a sketch of the original in the book I'm reading, which June gave me as a gift. To me, the figure looks like an alien with the body of a faun. Otto's is stand-alone, but in context the original appears with a flying saucer-looking thing above it.

What I find more fascinating than the mystery of cave art's meaning is the effort some artists apparently went through to create it, making dangerous journeys underground with stone lanterns, crawling and climbing through tight, cramped corridors to access hidden chambers, compelled, I assume, by some awesome vision. I envy them that. I wish I believed in something enough to follow it down into the darkness.

In the centre of Kuba's altar is a crude image of a naked figure drawn from behind walking toward a mountain. At the top of the mountain is a symbol. Next to the picture are four black and white photographs. I ask him who they are. "This is my teacher," he says, pointing to an Indian man. "And this," he says, pointing to another man, "is his student, the one who started the dances what we do. So they are my spiritual ancestors. And these are my family ancestors," he says, pointing to the other two pictures. "This is my grandmother and grandfather, and this is my other grandmother and grandfather."

I ask how he got involved with the dances.

"Oh, I told that story thousand times," he says, but he always answers my questions, and he never seems to mind that I have so many. "What attracted me was I first saw dances when I was eight years old, because my mother was interested in such things, and I was amazed adults are holding hands and singing in circles. And then many years later I saw dances when I was on an event in Prague, and I remembered from when I was a child, and I was like yes, this is exactly the tool what I'm looking for bringing people together and make them meet each other with some deeper purpose, not just a performance like what I was doing with Pavla, the special people on the stage, but actually everyone singing and dancing together. And during that dances, we danced one song what made me feel so safe. I didn't know what it is, but some time later I was on one ceremony, and someone sang this song, and I again felt huge power and safety, and I saw myself running naked between the trees and feeling happy and free, and there was hawk flying above me. I didn't speak much English in that time, but the hawk talked to me in English and said, *You're on the right path, but don't do unnecessary curves. Go straight to the goal.* I looked where the path was going, and it was going up to the hill, and on top the hill was this symbol." He points at the picture on his altar.

"And then I was going to the New Zealand camp first time, and everywhere was this symbol. I was like wow! And I loved that it's so nondogmatic and loving, and I loved that every single dance was from different tradition, and there was so much wisdom. It's not just a bunch of hippies singing in the circles in the gym. I see the culture where it comes from, and I can relate to the deep meaning of the things what we are doing, and I felt that as much I dance, and as much as I lead dances, it's making me softer and softer. So I felt like I arrived home."

"So you lead dances, too?"

"Of course," he says. "You didn't see me in New Zealand?"

"No," I say.

"Oh," he says. "So anyway important moment for me was when I first time came to India for celebration of the death of my teacher, and I expected that we would do dances there with people from all around the world, but when I arrived I learned there is, like I knew there were different names of different lineage, but there I got the message that there are many things what they don't agree on. They are quite divided. There is even some competition. And one woman from Holland told me, *And did you hear those Americans are coming this year to do their weird circle dancing again?* I was surprised. I said, *Oh, are they?*"

"Did you pretend not to know them?"

"I told her later, when we were more connected. But after that, I start to get messages that I should do something, because this division doesn't feel like the best. And when I was fasting and meditating, my teacher arrived right into my body and said, *I need your help. People are misusing the teachings what I brought. They are establishing churches about me, and it's total misunderstanding. Of course, because I was human I did it also for the fame of myself, but those people are still following it, and it's a mistake. You have big potential to make it humble and real and about freedom of the heart and the mind. This is your mission, and you have full support of us as the elders of this lineage to bring the transformation."*

"So that's your purpose?"

"I don't know," he says. He picks up the drawing from his altar. "Sometimes I feel like yes. I felt honoured. But on the other hand, I don't like how he was jumping into me and telling me what to do."

DURING THE DAY we talk, cook, make love. There are new dimensions every time. I ask him if he imagines doing things with me that we haven't done yet. We're naked in bed.

"Yes!" he says. "I imagine introducing you to my family and friends. I imagine us going on trips. Picking mushrooms, visiting Šumava, swimming on one very special place, and Velká Amerika, seeing the Cimrman play in English, I want to show you all the Svěrák movies, and Foglar . . ."

We have very few shared cultural references, so instead of discovering what we both love, I discover what he loves, and he loves when I love it. Surprisingly, what I love most are the songs. For all I know they're the same songs I hated as a child, but from him they are indescribably beautiful. I've started to request my favourites, and when he sings them for me I imagine myself as an old woman looking back on this with longing.

He tells me about his vision of a house in the country with a woodstove and children and a wife to drink thyme tea with in the evenings. He asks if I can imagine living in the bus, and I tell him I don't think so. I ask if he can imagine living outside of the Czech Republic, and he says maybe in New Zealand. I tell myself this is temporary, and that makes it feel easier.

The apartment I liked is taken. He asks me to stay with him longer. My main concern is the toilet. I can't relax without a door and with mice running under my feet, and I'm afraid of getting hantavirus. Still, I agree to stay. How can I not? I want to know what happens next.

WE'RE SITTING AT the piano on the landing. Kuba is playing a song I haven't heard before. Listening to him, watching his hands float over the keys, I find myself daydreaming about life in the cottage with the thyme tea. I imagine a stream, and two sweet children, and a stone wall in the garden.

"That's my new favourite," I say.

"That's Nohavica," he says. "Most of your favourite are Nohavica."

"It reminds me of Leonard Cohen."

"I heard Leonard Cohen is like Canadian Nohavica."

"Probably the other way around," I say. "What's it about?"

"It's sort of like a poetic expression of someone who is trying to talk to the . . . do you know the Halleyova kometa?"

"Halley's Comet?"

"Yes, so he see her and he want to sing a song to describe to her all the beauty and all the shits of humans and life on the earth. But he can't do it. His own uselessness stops him. But it's not uselessness, it's like when you want to do something, but it doesn't work. It will never work."

"Futility?"

"His own, this thing whatever it is, infility? It stops him. And he's sad he cannot manage it, but he knows even he will not be here any more when the comet fly around earth again, someone else will sing to her for sure."

Back in our room, he sits at the table and lights candles and incense while I make tea. "I was doing the research," he says. "I think we can contact to the department of . . . it's called the department of inner stuff?"

"Internal affairs?"

"Probably. Anyway, we can write there to ask them about finding the information about your family, and it's possible something will come back."

I've told him everything I know about my Czech family. They lived in České Budějovice—not Prague, as I told him the first time he asked—my mother's father was an alcoholic and died when my mother was twelve, my grandmother's name is Marie, like me, and my mother had an older brother named Jan, who died as a child after he fell off a roof.

Kuba is very keen for me to look for my relatives, especially my grandmother. I know I should be, too, but I'm not—maybe because I wouldn't trust my motivations, or maybe because I'm genuinely not interested. I did do a DNA test a few years ago, and there were some distant cousins with Czech names, but I didn't see why I should care about people who have a few percent of the same DNA as me more than I care about anyone else. And my mother never had anything nice to say about my grandmother. Actually, I don't remember her talking about her mother at all. It was my father who told me she was basically a pimp. He says she took my mother to work in a pub when my mother was fifteen, and she waited outside knowing my mother was having sex with men for money. He says she waited so she could get all the money my mother made, but I wonder if she stayed there to protect my mother. Either way, it's not great.

"And if something comes back?" I ask. "Then what?"

"You can decide," he says. "Maybe we can meet them? Or at least find where they are buried."

"I'm not sure I want to meet them," I say. "I don't think they're very nice people."

"If I was in such a situation, I would be interested no matter how they are," he says. "But your family had to have the courage to leave behind the homeland, so the detachment from them is probably still in you."

"And that's a bad thing?"

"You can get so much, Májenka. Years ago, I was going on the bike to Germany, and I intentionally went through the area where my grandfather was from. I asked the vicar in the church if he knows some people with my name, and he told me *when you continue in the direction of Germany, behind the next village watch out for the cross in the alley of the linden trees.* I went there and saw the cross from eighteenth century, and there was written that it was built by a man with my name. It actually changed a lot in me. I many times felt the lineage behind me, but it felt very sacred knowing that probably people who gave their best and their worst to my grandfather's life through their blood were walking those roads and those forests, and they were adoring the same views of the fields."

"So what do you suggest?"

"Well, first we write to the department of inner stuff."

I agree, mostly because it's so sweet that he cares.

"And what about to look for your mother's grave?" he asks. "Your father have to know where it is."

"It's in Vancouver," I say, and I hope he won't ask for details, because I've never visited.

"I thought she was in Czech Republic."

"My father says she kissed the ground before she crossed the border, but she never came back here."

"How it happened?"

"What?"

"How she left? It was not allowed in that time."

"She went on a youth tour to Yugoslavia and left the group when they were refueling in Austria."

"She had to have such a courage, Mája."

I nod, but the truth is I've never thought of her that way.

"I wanted to ask you," he says. "How long will you stay here?"

Oh my God, does he want to get rid of me? Does he think I'm a monster for not caring about my family? "I'm not sure," I say. "Why?"

"For example, will you come to India with me on February?"

"Kuba, we don't even know if we want to live in the same country."

"I feel like the little child who is afraid to be left," he says. Then he starts to cry in a way I have never seen a man cry before, but I don't feel awkward. "I never opened myself to someone like this," he says. "It was from when I first time saw you. I was saying, *Here I am. Please love me.*"

He pulls a tissue from a box on the table, and when he blows his nose, blood comes out. "It's happening when I'm over-warmed," he says.

"It's not that I don't have feelings, you know. I'm a Cancer." I put my hands over my head. "I go into my shell."

"What? You have cancer?"

"I *am* a Cancer. The crab. Like in the zodiac?"

"Ah, yes," he says. "Rak."

"What are you?"

"I'm the schizophrenic one made of two."

"Gemini. The twins."

"Mhm. Like me and you. Did you notice it? We are like a twins. I'm the naughty one, and you are also the naughty one."

"At least we have that in common."

"Sing me one song," he says.

"I don't sing."

He makes a pleading face, so I say the words to Daisy Bell. When I've finished, he says, "Májenka, would you like to meet your ancestors with me?"

"What does that mean?"

"Would you like to go to the forest and ask our ancestors to be with us?"

"I'm not sure I want to be with them."

"Why?"

"Well, on my mother's side I don't know anything about them. And on my father's side they were missionaries, so they went to other people's countries and tried to make them believe what they believed, took their land, and bulldozed their cultures."

"I believe we have support from them to not only not do the same mistakes what they did, but also to help to address the injustices what they were part of," he says. "And they are incredible source of life energy and wisdom."

"Why are they a better source of wisdom than, I don't know, your grandmother?"

"Because they don't have to deal with the material world obstacles. And it's good to not be alone, Májenka. We all carry the pain of our ancestors who had to suffer so much and do so much mistakes, but my interaction with my ancestors is with the only intention to celebrate, and to know we are not alone for whatever we are going through. You can lean back, and they hold you. You can see the direction and go, and you don't go alone. There's a never-ending pyramid of beings going with you. And you may have whatever philosophy or intellectual ideas, but you can't compare to that knowledge."

"But what if the messages you hear from them are just voices in your own head?"

"I do what I trust in," he says. "And I trust that this is wider picture than what we can experience in daily life, and it's worth to maintain these relationships and to communicate. And it doesn't mean listen and adore it with no doubts. But have it as lifetime relationship, also with attitude that it's not only that I will suck something from them, but also that I can be open door to the embodied world on the earth planet, and what healing I do now is also healing them into the past."

"Can I ask you a question?" I ask.

"Of course."

"Do you have other lovers?"

He holds the tissue to his nose. "There was one what I thought it could be something."

"Yes."

"Before I was leaving to New Zealand, I met one other Mája with same eyes what you have, and also writer. I was confused, because I felt there something, and at that time my life was full of signs, but when I met her more I knew she was not in the energies what I am looking for. Then when I met you on New Zealand

I was asking if I feel something to you because you remind me her, but when I remember how I know you from two years before, I got that it was opposite. I felt something to her because she remind me you."

"Did you have a relationship with her?"

"No," he says. "Just meeting in a tea room." I make a skeptical face. "Májenka moje," he says. "If you think that after experiencing the connection what we have I am still thinking about anyone else, you are really dummy."

"And are there others?"

"No. Not others."

"And what were the energies you were looking for?"

"You," he says.

"Meaning?"

"You, girl. Gorgeous woman with brown eyes. And such a boobs!" He grabs my breasts. "If I am woman, and I have such a weapons, I would use it every day, but you are hiding it in your big sweaters."

I start to unbutton his jeans, and he puts the bloody tissue aside. From next door, we can hear Otto singing along to the same mantra he plays on repeat day and night: *om mani padme hum om mani padme hum.*

AT DUSK, WE walk to the forest. I carry two of his deerskin drums, and he carries two overtone flutes and a full backpack. Our neighbour, an elderly woman, calls to us out of her window and gives Kuba a dripping jar of honey with the comb inside. We say dobrý den to the people we pass. I was saying ahoj to everyone until Kuba told me it's extremely informal, and I shouldn't say it to strangers or the elderly.

When we pass the pub at the highway, we stop to talk to some men drinking outside. Kuba tells me they're his friends from his former life as a punk musician, which is hard to imagine.

"I asked them how they are," he says. "They were all complaining. *Always in the job.* Some people never smile in the life. But I love them. That's what I'm realising when I'm on my travels. I come back and see such a miserable faces, and I feel like it's awful, but it's mine."

In the forest, we climb up to a flat rock overlooking a dark brown stream. There's a fireplace in the centre of the rock and candles perched on the mossy rockface behind us. Kuba takes things out of his bag, lights the candles, and starts to prepare the fire. He does this all slowly, and not in a way that invites me to help. When he lights the fire, he takes a hawk wing out of his bag and uses it to fan the flames.

"I am greeting you the spirits and guards of this place," he says. "My name is Jakub, and this is Mája, and we are asking for your guidance and support in our intention for Mája to experience the wisdom of her ancestors." He looks at me. "Do you want to say something?"

"I don't know what to say."

He closes his eyes. I wonder if he's contemplating what a dud I am and wishing he'd gone with the other Mája. He takes a rattle from his backpack, picks up a frame drum, and taps the rattle against the drum as he makes sounds like *sh-sh-sh-sh-sh-sh*.

He passes me the other drum and a rattle. "I will invite my ancestors to the dance," he says. "And when they are present, if we feel like, let's invite yours also. My ancestors would be dancing on my side, and your ancestors, if they appear, will join on your side."

He drums in a simple rhythm and takes small steps from side to side. At first it's gentle and slow, but it gets louder and faster. As I watch him, I try to work out what would be worse—if I don't see anything and admit it or if I don't see anything and pretend I did.

"Do you want to invite your ancestors now?" he says.

"Okay."

"So do the same what I do," he says. I gently shake the rattle and step from side to side, but I can't bring myself to play the drum.

"And now," he says, "we want to invite, if it is in harmony with the ancestors of Mája, please come and dance here with us, and let's celebrate together the presence and the greatness of life and existence."

I imagine my faceless grandparents on my mother's side, the missionaries on my father's, sailing from England full of certitude. Or were they as lost as I am? And if I have descendants, will they want to have a relationship with me, or will they only feel ashamed of what I've done and failed to do? I imagine my children's children's children in a forest in the future trying to reach back to me, and I feel touched, but I'm not sure how real it is, because I want Kuba to know that I'm touched, that I'm capable of that.

When it's over, he's in no rush to leave. He takes a hot water bottle out of his backpack and fills it with water from his thermos, then he gives it to me and wraps me in a blanket.

"What else do you have in there?" I ask.

"Everything," he says. "It's the box of what everyone need, every Scout. You have there little knife, tiny little spoon, aspirin, plasters, light, hot water bottle, blankie, your beloved's favourite dried mango, tampons, probiotics."

I've never met anyone so thoughtful and so prepared. He's found Czech equivalents of my supplements and probiotics. He helps me to read all the labels at the supermarket, and he never complains or questions me about my weird diet. Everything I like he buys in bulk, he's constantly surprising me with gifts, and I have to insist that he lets me help pay for things, which I admit is kind of nice after years of carefully splitting bills with Drew.

He sits behind me, and I lean into him and close my eyes. "Did you see anything?" he asks.

"No. Did you?"

"I saw very clear images of thousands of feet doing exactly the movements as I did," he says. "But when we invited your ancestors, I didn't see anything. I knew there was a presence, but it was very narrow if you compare with the big crowd of souls dancing with me. It was something very misty, and it felt like it's not the smooth connection between you and them."

"What can I do about that?"

"If you believe, and you see the sense in it, maintain your relationship with them."

"How?"

"The first is, you have to trust in your abilities to connect."

"So I only have to believe in it and it will work?"

"I think so."

"And you totally believe in it?"

"I don't only believe, I have a proof, because I did this with people who never believed in anything spiritual, and through dancing with the ancestors they were meeting their beloveds, their grandmothers, and grandfathers, and parents, and some people were getting crazy. That's why I never repeat it in the groups, because I felt I'm opening worlds which I don't really understand, and I don't know how to create safe space to deal with the consequences, but I can do it for you because I know you would not get crazy."

"How do you know?"

"Because you are super grounded woman, lásko."

"What's lásko?"

He kisses my cheek. "Love," he says. He pulls me down onto the dirt and rocks with him. "You see?" he says. "Grounded."

KUBA MESSAGES THE distant cousins with Czech names in my DNA matches to ask if they've heard of my family. He gets me to write down all the details I know about my family members, and he sends an email to the department of inner stuff to ask if they have any records that we can access. He says my mother's family name is one of the most common in the Czech Republic, but if we trust in it, it will work. I don't know if I trust in the department of inner stuff, but I think I trust in Kuba.

When we get back from the post office, I make dinner, and he sings me all of my favourite songs. Kometa, Přijdu hned, V půl osmé, Nad stádem koní, Slunovrat. It's so sad that most people will never hear these songs, and I feel so lucky to be discovering them, but it's also confusing, because I can't tell where the line is between my feelings for Kuba and my feelings for this music.

When he's gone through all my requests, he sings a song that stirs up a memory of my mother singing me to sleep in my bedroom in Vancouver. I ask him what it's about.

"That's Czech national hymn," he says.

"What do the words mean?"

"It's like, where is my home? Where is my home? The water is humming? Not humming but, fizzing? Rushing? Just the sound of the river rushing down the meadows. The pine trees are growing on the rocks and sh-shing in the wind. In the orchard—this is such an old language, so I don't even know how to translate it—pops up? Or in the orchard, um, the blossom of the spring appears. It looks like the paradise on the earth. And that is that gorgeous country. Czech country. My home. Czech country. My home."

"That's lovely."

"Yes," he says. "And it's quite unique, because most of the national hymns are about the God and war and things like that, but our one is about the landscape."

It makes me realise how myopic my view of this place has been. Maybe it's because my inner child is angry that my mother loved linden trees more than me, but since I've been here I've been so focused on Kuba I haven't taken in my surroundings at all.

HE SHOWS ME his schedule and tells me more about the places he's going, events he's leading or participating in. Honestly, it sounds terrifying, and I'm feeling more and more unwell. It's not anything in particular, just a general feeling of unease, and I keep losing weight. I've been extra careful about my diet, so my skin is okay, but my tongue feels weird, and I'm still having the shaking walls and something-is-coming dreams.

"So do you know what you would like to join?" he asks.

"Can I decide later?"

"Everything what you want, my love. But at least you will come for dances in the forest day after tomorrow? I organise it for you."

I guess this is his life, and we can't stay in this room forever.

"And also frog," he says. "I already subscribed us there."

"Frog?"

"It's healing about the frog from the rainforest. They sing the song what attract the frog and get them from the trees and collect their secretion."

"Uh huh."

"So it let go some secrete from its body, and they burn you on some certain place, then they put into the wound little piece of the medicine."

"Who does?" I ask.

"Libuše."

"She's Czech?"

"Yes," he says.

"And is she trained, or?"

"She went many times to South America for the trainings."

"And what will happen to us?"

"In most cases people vomit a lot," he says. "And it can take one hour or two hours, then you eat. You have nice soup!"

"And why would we do this?"

"It get rid of the parasite, and it helps with the immunity, and after you feel very clean."

I do want to feel clean.

"What about the frogs?" I ask. "Do they kill them?"

"No," he says. "They go back to their homes."

I know I said I would say yes to everything, but this one's going to require some research. "Can I think about it?" I ask.

"Of course," he says. "What about your writing, love?"

"What about it?"

"You are writer, and I don't know anything about your writing."

I can't tell him about my abortive novel, because I don't want him to know what a failure I am. I can't tell him about my grant application, either, because I don't want him to think I'm here gathering material. I'll say something about writing in general, and what it means to me. "Well," I start.

He takes out his phone and says, "Sorry, I have to answer." Then he walks away saying, "Prosím, tady Jakub."

When he gets back, I tell him I find it rude to answer the phone in the middle of a conversation. "I'm sorry about it," he says. "I am getting hundreds of phone calls and emails what I don't answer, but this was important. I will try not to repeat it."

Now I feel bad. He's taken all this time out of his busy life to host me, he's so thoughtful of my needs, and I'm getting on his case because he answered the phone.

"No, I'm sorry," I say. I don't even want to talk about writing.

"Don't apologise, my love," he says. "There is nothing wrong on you."

He asks me to sing him a song. Instead I recite The Lady of Shalott, which is almost as awkward as singing. I remember reading somewhere that it's about female empowerment—the woman locked away doing crafts defies the codes of Victorian femininity—but I prefer the interpretation that she represents the artist using art to keep the world at a safe distance. Anyway, the ending doesn't exactly encourage women or artists to come down from their towers.

When I've finished he says, "It's beautiful. I don't understand half of it, but it's beautiful."

I would be very surprised if he understood half of it.

I CHECKED THE genealogy website to see if any of my distant cousins had responded to our message. Nothing yet. June emailed to tell me that Sarie died. I told Kuba and he cried even though he never met the dog. "Why am I always the one weeping?" he said. He didn't mean it as a criticism. I do find it sad that Sarie died, but mostly I hope it wasn't my fault.

I've never seen my father cry, and I can only remember one occasion when I saw my mother cry from something other than physical pain. When I was six, Teta Běta started preparing me for my Confirmation and First Communion. After Teta died, my mother took over as my teacher, but instead of telling me that I was tainted by original sin and being constantly surveilled by someone who could read my mind, she gave me pictures of Bible stories to colour in while she asked questions and I answered in the prescribed way:

"Who made you?"

"God made me."

"Why did God make you?"

"To know Him, to love Him, to serve Him, and be happy with Him for all eternity."

One day after our lesson, she gave me a gift wrapped in silver paper and tied with a blue satin bow. Inside was a white silk dress, a white veil and gloves, and a white handkerchief embroidered with a blue cross and a border of blue letters reading, *For I am the Lord your God who takes hold of your right hand and says to you, Do not be afraid; I will help you.*

I had assumed that the God Teta Běta taught me about was the same one my mother believed in, but that handkerchief showed me that, like me, my mother saw God as her friend, and my relief made me cry. When I looked at my mother, I saw that she was crying, too.

She didn't pick me up from school the next day. At first my father was furious. His documentary had been nominated for an award, and he'd had to leave an interview to come and get me. Later his anger turned to worry, and then back to anger when he discovered she'd taken most of our savings.

Gina came to stay with us until my father could figure out what to do. She says I stopped eating and refused to go to school, but I don't remember that. What I remember is being certain my mother was coming back, because she wouldn't miss my First Communion.

WE CLIMB THE hill in the forest and sit by the spent fire. He's behind me with his arms around me. I'm staring at the veins and tendons in his forearms. He's flawless, like a statue.

"Becca says you hypnotised me," I say.

He laughs. "Yes, I'm the magician who hypnotised you."

"What should I do then?"

"What I tell you."

"I thought you were so pure when I met you."

"You thought I was the angel?"

"Yes."

"I am," he says.

A figure appears at the bottom of the hill, marching through the trees. Kuba makes a bird sound, and Otto turns and salutes, then keeps marching.

"What's he doing?"

"He's doing patrol to make sure people are not cutting down trees or frightening animals with motorcycles."

Once I peeked into his room when he was out. I felt I had to know what was in there if I was going to live next door to it. The floor is concrete speckled with paint, there are several feeding stations for mice, and all of the walls are decorated with paintings and knife scrawls of words, figures, and symbols.

"Why does he have those statues everywhere?" I ask.

"Which ones?"

"Those things with the spears through them."

"He loves the aliens," Kuba says.

"So they're aliens?"

"He think so," Kuba says. "He saw quite a few times aliens, and he is doing the art according the old cave paintings art. He's studying it and watching all the YouTube clips, and he's preparing the special costume. He has the altar, and he is looking forward they will arrive, and he doesn't want to be not prepared for it."

"Do you believe in aliens?" I ask.

"I don't have any proof, but it somehow feels foolish to think we are the only ones in the universe. What about you?"

I tell him the book I'm reading is making me consider the possibility that they exist, but I don't think they are necessarily our friends.

"But is Otto okay?" I ask.

"He is tough but extremely sensitive inside," Kuba says. "Once I arrived from somewhere, and I saw him standing on the garden, and I said what's happening, and he said nehoda, which means the accident. Then I realised he is weeping, and he was still repeating *terrible accident happened.* You know he doesn't use the shower because he doesn't want to waste the water, so when I was having some concerts far away or when I travelled, no one was using the water, and the mouse was trapped there, and she died."

"That's why the *Become a Buddha* sign?"

"He wants them to be free."

"And he really has a costume for the aliens?"

"I never saw it," Kuba says. "But I think it's real because he is not lying." He takes a plastic bag out of his backpack, looks inside and then at me.

"I need to ask if I can use her parts," he says.

"Oh God, the owl? Isn't it rotten?"

He says, "The weather was cold, lásko," and for the first time I sense impatience in his voice. He pulls the carcass out of the bag with his bare hands. I move away. He speaks to the bird in Czech, then he holds up his drum and taps it with his rattle. His eyes are closed, and he makes little movements. I watch, studying him. It takes a long time, but eventually the rhythm changes, and soon after that he opens his eyes and bows.

After what feels like a respectful silence, I ask him what happened.

"I got clear message," he says. "She wants me to use her wings. I keep one for me, and I am supposed to give second one to owners of the land where we will live in the bus."

It's the first time he's brought up the bus since I told him I don't want to live there. Does he think I've changed my mind? Have I? There's something thrilling about the idea of giving my life over to his visions, probably because I don't have any of my own any more.

"What did you see?" I ask.

"There were owls spinning in the circles around me and you. We were holding each other, and they were stroking us and saying we are supposed to clean a lot together. Then I saw complete owl as it was, the shape of it in the light. And I see there are missing feathers and one wing, and I consciously bring that energy, it's like the light shade of the feathers and wing, I bring it back and attach it to the owl body. So the spirit is exactly in the shape how it was when it died."

"Oh my God, Kuba. We're so different."

"No, we are the same," he says. "And I am becoming more as you are, and you are becoming more as I am."

I DREAMT I had been abducted by aliens, and I was pregnant with a hybrid alien-human baby. It was dying, and I had to open my stomach to let it breathe. Becca was with me. My stomach was open, and the baby's head was out. There was also a cat in there that was sliced open along its stomach. Then the baby jumped out. Becca screamed and tried to put it back in, but it didn't work. The cat also came out and was walking away. I was shouting at Becca to stop it, because its insides were falling out. I got the baby and held it to my breast. I was thinking it would be totally traumatised by what had happened, but then it smiled at me, and I was happy that it knew me. My breasts were crusty from milk, and there was milk all around the baby's mouth and face. I asked Becca to get something to clean it with, and she said, "Get it yourself. You can still move around with a baby." I felt alone and abandoned. No baby shower, no magical birth. I decided I was going to try to escape with the baby, but I didn't have anything. No car seat, no diaper bag, no baby! I looked around. The baby was asleep in a crib in the corner. I stared at it and thought my feelings were all wrong, and I should write a Facebook post about how much I loved it, but really what I felt was mostly horror and a crushing sense of responsibility, because I had to save it somehow. While I was thinking that, it woke up and started spinning around like a wind-up toy. It spun off through the bars of the crib and landed on the floor in a pile of plastic. I put it back together. I think it was a merry-go-round. I put it back in the crib.

I need to find some new reading material. The book I'm reading inspired me to Google alien abduction narratives, and I was up until two a.m. devouring first-hand accounts, wondering if I might be a repeat abductee myself with screen memories implanted to account for missing time. It would explain a lot.

Kuba is downstairs. I can hear something frying and the kettle boiling. There's a fresh hot water bottle next to me. Over breakfast, he tells me he had an answer from the department of inner stuff telling him to forward his email about my family to "the matrix" in České Budějovice, which he has now done. I thank him and get up to go to the toilet.

"Lásko, I also want to say I actually notice that you are probably not familiar with this European system of door handles?" he says. I raise my eyebrows. "They actually work the way that you can close the door without sound, so if you can just put the lever down and close it and then put the lever up it would actually not do any sound." He's demonstrating this with hand gestures. "And uh, so you don't need to smash the door any time you walk through the room?" He smiles. "Especially when someone is sleeping in the room." He reaches for my hand and kisses it.

At the door I say, "We do have door knobs in Canada, you know?" I close the door behind me, holding the handle down first, then open it again and say, "And New Zealand."

WE FILL THE van with instruments and drive to the forest, where a group of people are gathered. When they see Kuba's van, some of them stop what they're doing and come over to where we've parked. I don't want to get out. Why? It's a sunny day, and these are Kuba's friends. Why is my body reacting as if I was surrounded by wolves?

A brunette hugs Kuba. He says, "Nazdar!" and lifts her off the ground. When he puts her down, they stare at each other, then she comes to me, takes my hands, and gives me this super sincere, wide-eyed stare. "I feel you like a sister," she says.

Her name is Šárka. She has perfect skin and seems altogether angelic. Kuba is behind her. I tell her my name. She says, "I know. I know a lot about you." He puts his arms around her and holds her from behind. She puts her hands on his hands. This is normal for them. This is normal. And she seems lovely. Someone says something to her in Czech. She touches my cheek with the back of her hand, and I flinch, because I hate people touching my face. She says, "We can talk later."

Kuba goes to tune his instruments. Everyone seems to have a role—setting up tables, building a fire, chopping wood. Three men are using scythes to cut the grass in the clearing where we will be dancing.

I pick up an axe and a piece of wood, but before I can put the wood on the chopping block, a man takes the axe, leans it against a stump, and hugs me. I have no idea what it means. I feel exhausted. I want to go back to the house and sleep, back to Canada and sleep. But why? Nothing bad is happening. People are being nice to me. Why can't I be normal and enjoy things?

I join some women who are breaking small twigs off a pile of branches. They acknowledge me but don't say anything, and I'm grateful to be able to do something without interacting with anyone. I look around for Kuba and see him talking to some men. They're all laughing.

Once everything is set up, we make a circle. Kuba and I are on opposite sides, but he comes and puts his arm around my waist. As he explains the dance, he translates for me, and I love the feeling of being next to him and belonging to him. Then he asks Šárka to be his partner so he can demonstrate the dance. Watching them together makes me feel queasy, so I compose an email to Becca in my head. I'll tell her about how awkward it was when we arrived. I'll describe the look Šárka gave me. I'll call it cult face.

After a while we take a break, and people go to do some kind of cleansing ritual in the stream. I sit alone on the grass, and like in junior high school, the longer I sit on my own, the more I'm convinced that no one likes me, including me. When it's time to meet around the fire for whatever's happening next, I have the beginnings of a migraine, so I excuse myself, walk back to the house, lie in bed with my head under a pillow, and try to sort through my feelings. What I arrive at is this: I've organised my entire adult life so that I don't have to feel how I felt today, but being here is showing me what a neurotic freak I still am under the persona I cultivated after I went to university and learned to act normal. I need to face that if I want to be a real adult, and like Gina says, "As soon as you decide to change something, the universe offers you a test."

Kuba comes home after midnight. I'm so tired, and my head still hurts, but when he lies down next to me, I turn to him. I need more of him. I feel like I'll never have enough.

He buries his face in my breasts. He smells of campfire and something herbal.

"Have you ever been intimate with Šárka?" I ask.

"Don't talk to me," he says. "I'm suiciding myself."

I push him away. "Have you?"

"What?"

"Have you been intimate with Šárka?"

"Which Šárka?"

"From today."

"What means intimate."

"Have you had sex with her?"

"You are so sexy," he says. He has an annoying habit of answering questions with jokes or compliments. What time is it? *Time for a cuddles!* Do you want some soup? *How can anyone live without you?*

I ask again, and he says no.

"What about the other women who were there today?" I hate that I'm asking, and I hate that he has to think about it before he answers, but he says no.

"Will you tell me if we're meeting women you've had relationships with?"

"Of course, lásko. There are not so many."

"She said she knew a lot about me."

He stretches and yawns. "Who?"

"Šárka."

"I'm writing always about the progress what I have on my journeys," he says. "And you are the best experience what I had in my last travels, so everyone knows."

That's so sweet. I feel bad for grilling him.

"Did you write an email or what?"

"A blog."

"You have a blog where you write about me?"

"Not now, a traveller blog."

"What did you write?"

"I wrote that I met you, and I had a very rich time with you, and it was unique and unexpected connection, and it was hard to say goodbye. And also that I'm very much hoping we will see each other again in Europe." He snuggles into me and rubs his nose against my neck. "Sing me one song," he says.

"I don't sing."

"Yes you do! All the day you are . . ." He hums a tune.

"It's involuntary."

"You are the hummingbird," he says. He kisses me. "How was your sex with Drew?" he asks.

"What?" I say. "Not what I want to talk about. How about you?"

"My sex with Drew was never good," he says. I roll my eyes. He says, "My last partner, Liliana, didn't know about gentleness. She was peeling me as a potato."

I put my nose in his hair. "What is that smell?"

"That's the mateřídouška. In English it's the thyme. That's the only one poem I know off the cuff. It was the must. You have to learn it in the primary school."

"Tell me then." I turn around, and he cuddles me and whispers into my ear.

"So woman died," he says. "Mother died, and her kids were left behind, they were abandoned." He pauses. "But they were coming every morning on the grave and searching for their mum. And the mercy of the mum towards the kids embodied her into small flower, which kids called mateřídouška, the breath of the mother. They recognised her by the smell, and they celebrated. Then the speaker is saying Dear Thyme, you who are beloved to our land, the ancestor of the . . . history fairy tales? If there is Greek?"

"Myth?"

"Yes. Oh myth of Czech Slavic tribe, I will collect you into the humble . . . bundle? If you come to the lady and you kneel in front of . . ."

"Bouquet."

"Yes. I will collect you and I will spread you all over the country to the far, far fields where you have your relatives. And I hope that some daughters will find you, which will like your breath, and I hope that some sons will find you, because you show them your heart. So it's like support to the future generations. To the daughters the breath, and to the young men the heart of the mum."

I turn and face him again. I'm getting used to looking into his eyes.

"You are so beautiful being," he says. "One man told me today, your new girlfriend is so beautiful, it's hard to look at her. I told him, you know why is she so beautiful? Because I invented her."

EVERY DAY IS filled with activity. We're always going somewhere new, meeting new people, and like a child, I rarely have a sense of where we are. I haven't looked at a map once.

We went to a factory to get skins for a frame drum-making workshop. We had lunch in a courtyard at a Hare Krishna restaurant. He took me to Prague Castle and the Orangery and told me about the important role defenestration (i.e., throwing people out of windows) has played in Czech history. I met his mother, who is jolly and affectionate and speaks about three words of English, and his father, who spent most of our visit smoking and silently shelling walnuts. We had a campfire in the backyard with some of his childhood friends, who are all very nice and excellent musicians, especially his best friend, Ondra.

He took me on a tour of the city that began by the Vltava River at Kampa Island and ended at the top of a TV tower in Žižkov. He took me to a church behind Václavské náměstí, where we knelt in the pews kind of as a joke, but I did say a little prayer of gratitude. We went to see a band called Hradišťan. He took me to the cemetery at Vyšehrad and laughed at how I pronounce Dvořák. He showed me where his maternal grandparents and great grandparents are buried. He set a bundle of thyme on their grave, put his arm around me and said, "This is Mája. I love her."

He heard back from the matrix. They said they can only release information to confirmed family members, so I have to go there and prove my identity. I asked Gina to send me a certified copy of my birth certificate, and she wrote Kuba a long email thanking him for encouraging me to connect with my past.

Now we're taking the train to Velká Amerika, an abandoned limestone quarry outside of Prague where there's an underground system of manmade caves. "And each cave have a name," Kuba says. "And they are full of batbirds? Batman?"

"Bats."

"And in past people would pack their US military packs and go tramping there, being brothers and sisters, travelling in the trains, and all the coaches were singing. And they weared all military clothes from different armies, so it looked like the Soviet Army is going together in the train with the US Army and the Bundeswehr, and they were sleeping together under the stars by the fires."

That lizard poster I stood next to when I arrived at the train station is all over Prague. There's one in our carriage. The text says *Něco Přichází: 01.11.15.* I ask Kuba what it means. He says, "It means something is . . . nearing? Or something is coming." Fucking hell that's creepy, but I know it's an ad for a giant lizard movie, not a personal warning from the universe.

When we get off the train, we walk past a castle and along a forest path, then over a railway track to a lookoff into the deep quarry, Velká Amerika, so named, Kuba says, because people thought it looked like a canyon in the American West. We have a picnic, walk back across a meadow, and climb a hill to where Kuba, Ondra, and their other friend slept outside together for the first time and named their tribe, Huambisa.

"It was the biggest day of our lives," he says. "We were making the buřty on the fire and we all said this is the best buřty ever. We were so excited."

"Where did you get the name Huambisa?" I ask.

"It's a tribe in Amazonia what I learned about from our tourist club."

I ask what a tourist club is, and he explains that it's a club for families who meet in Prague's suburbs to plan trips into the wilderness. "And highlight of the year was three weeks long camp by Tatra Mountains," he says. "We hike to the empty meadow and build our kitchen, dig our toilets, clean our well, we had to maintain the little bridges, we built the sauna, and Scout tents for sleeping, and we lived there for three weeks, making the fires, singing the songs and going through the challenges. We had to do everything on our own. I'm sure it would be illegal now."

We stop by a hidden stone platform in the forest, and he shows me a tree with the word Huambisa carved into its trunk.

I ask what happened to his other friend, and Kuba says he died in a car crash with his father. "They were moving to make the space for a big truck, and the side of the road was too soft for the speed," he says. "So that was the end of Huambisa."

"KWAK KWAK." I open my eyes. He's standing at the top of the ladder.

"Frogs say ribbit."

"Czech frogs say kwak."

We've been fasting since morning, and I must have fallen asleep.

He's already packed my hot water bottle, a bottle of drinking water for each of us, a soft blanket, and the heart-shaped pillow with arms he bought for me at IKEA. On the way, we find a dead woodpecker on the road, and he prays for it before burying it under a tree. For the rest of the drive, he sings what I call Slovakian shouting songs, and I learn the word ovečky: sheep. A lot of the shouting songs are about sheep.

A young woman opens the door to a flat where a dozen people are spread out on mattresses along three walls of an unfurnished room. Along the fourth wall is an altar where some kind of wood is burning. A beautiful woman, maybe mid-forties with waist-length brown hair, heavy eye makeup, and noisy jewellery, jangles over and hugs Kuba. She's wearing a long skirt and a draping blouse. He kisses the top of her head.

Her name is Véra. He introduces us, and she says, "It's beautiful for me that you are here."

I say, "It's beautiful to be here," and I cringe at myself, because that's not something I would say.

Kuba sits between Véra and me. The woman leading the ceremony talks for a while, and Kuba translates. Her helper puts a red bucket in front of each of us, then the woman calls us to her altar one at a time. Kuba is first. He kneels in front of her, and they stare at each other. She says something to him and touches his chest. He takes off his shirt, and she takes what looks like a stick of incense and presses it into his skin six times in a vertical line along his sternum.

I'm next. I want to ask her if her little sticks are sterile, but I don't. We stare at each other, and I force myself not to look away or swallow. She touches the back of my neck. "I will make three points here," she says. "Is it okay?"

The burns don't hurt much at first, but the pain gets worse while I'm waiting for the next part.

Once she's finished burning everyone, she walks around the room, and sounds follow her. Some people breathe heavily. Some moan. The noises get louder. It's my turn. She uses a stick to put the poison into the burns on my neck.

First it stings. Then I feel heat in my stomach, which moves up into my chest. Someone vomits. I'm trying not to panic.

"Drink," the woman says. I lift my water and try to drink, but after one sip I vomit bubbly bile into my bucket. "Keep drinking," she says. I take another sip and vomit again. "Drink all," she says. People are vomiting and moaning. Someone is crying. But Kuba is still sitting straight-backed with his eyes closed, occasionally lifting his water and drinking from the side of his mouth.

I hold my hand over my heart and breathe in. The heat is so intense now. The woman leans down close to my face. She's singing. She holds a smoking piece of wood under my nose, and the smell makes me vomit again.

Kuba holds his bucket at arm's length and vomits so violently that it sprays out of the bucket onto him, Véra, and me. I wipe my face with my blanket, fall back onto my mattress, and pull my heart-shaped pillow under my head. I'm completely empty, too tired to even think. The woman looks into my bucket and makes sounds of approval, as if she can see everything there is to know about me in there, and it's all okay.

WE'RE AT A festival. I don't know where he is. For a while I walked around checking out the food stalls, and now I'm sitting on the grass in front of the stage. The man next to me is holding a comically-large frame drum. He greeted me in English. Can they tell by looking at me?

"That's a big drum," I say. "Are you going to perform?"

He seems annoyed by my question. "I will be leading a ritual," he says.

"Do you do similar things to, do you know Jakub . . ."

"Do you know Tesco?" he asks.

"The supermarket?"

He says, "I'm like Tesco, and Kuba is more like Penny Market."

He goes to do his ritual, and I lie in the grass and watch people dancing. Since I've been here, I've become very aware of a certain type of woman. I call them peacocks, even though it makes no sense zoologically. Normally I admire women who dress beautifully and seem comfortable in their skin, women like Véra. But these women I don't admire. I don't think I envy them, either, or if I do it's different than the kind of envy I'm used to— not that I wish I was more like them, but that I think they would make more sense with Kuba than I do. I often get the feeling that they think so, too.

Yesterday he led dances in České Budějovice. We went there to show my birth certificate and passport at a government office so we could file our application for information about my family, and Kuba organised an event in the evening, because he likes to have every waking moment filled with people, movement, music.

After visiting the government office, we went to a cemetery and looked at the graves. Neither of us said so, but I think we were both wondering if we were going to stumble upon my family members there. Then we went to the town square, where there's a Baroque fountain depicting Samson astride a lion. We had lunch in a café, walked through a park. He asked if I wanted to do a small ceremony to acknowledge my ancestors. Before I met him, I don't think there was a single ceremony in my life, apart from my baptism.

"Maybe you would like to bury a letter for them, or sing a song," he said. "It's not so important what it is. It's about the act. It can release the souls, and at the same time it can release the grief from you."

I told him I'd rather not. I can't do something like that unless I'm sure I mean it.

At the dances in the evening, all of the participants were women. Véra was there, and a gorgeous peacock-type named Marie, who I thought might be his other Mája. He was in the middle playing his guitar, and we were dancing in a circle around him. Watching him, it occurred to me that being with him is like holding something very bright very close to your face, but actually he's just a guy, and we have so little in common.

When he taught us the steps to the dance, it reminded me of *The Unbearable Lightness of Being,* how the female protagonist had a nightmare where she was forced to march naked around a pool with other women while her lover was suspended above them, shouting orders. When Kuba said, "free dancing," the women all did sexy, flowing movements, and I watched him watching them, especially Marie. Meanwhile, I walked around the circle making small gestures with my hands, wishing for it to be over.

After the dancing, Kuba had us split into couples to share. Marie went for Kuba, but an older woman with spiky white hair got to him first. Véra took my hand, and we went to the corner and sat facing each other. She told me her ex-husband, Tadeáš— who is also a dance leader—cheated on her and left her for a younger woman, and she feels angry all the time. I admired her honesty, and I decided that when it was my turn I would tell her the truth, which is that I'm not well, and I hate my skin, and I have no idea what I'm doing with my life. But when my turn came, I lost my courage. "I'm fine," I said. "I feel good with Kuba. It's overwhelming sometimes, but I'm grateful."

She held my hands and said, "I feel you."

As usual, it took ages for us to leave, because Kuba sees leaving not as an action, but as a period of time—almost an event in itself. The spiky white-haired woman hugged him *forever*. When he finally pulled away, she was weeping. He bowed to her. He wanted to invite everyone to come to dinner with us, but I asked if we could be alone. We went to an Indian restaurant, and while we were waiting for our food to arrive, he said, "It's interesting how you dance. It's so different from others."

"What do you mean?"

"Some people are so deeply into it . . . and you do the movements and have the open eyes, and I don't see any . . . prožívání. Like experiencing it intensely."

"Don't compare me to your harem," I said. I was surprised by how bitter I sounded, and I could tell that he was too.

"I don't have harem," he said.

"I don't like being compared," I said.

"I'm sorry you felt compared, Májenka. You see it's about my programmes. I felt that you don't like the dances, it's nothing special for you, it's boring. That's why I said it. I wanted you to tell me how you like it."

But I don't like it. I couldn't tell him that, though. I asked him if Marie was the other Mája he told me about. The one who looked like me, who he thought he might want to be with before he met me.

"No, it was not her," he said. "She is not coming for dances."

"I don't understand why you aren't with one of those women," I said.

"Which women?"

"All these goddesses who are so into what you do. Why not be with one of them?"

"Because I want you," he said. "You are the person what I was waiting for my whole life."

"I'm sorry," I said. "It's about my programmes, too. My father always had a lot of women around him, and he used to compare me to other girls my age."

"So good you can see it," he said.

"What's the deal with that woman who was hugging you for so long?"

"Barbora?"

"The older woman with the short white hair."

"She never lets go," he said. "She likes to hug forever. Not only me."

"Does she cry over everyone?"

"Once I had a feeling we may be somehow connected from ancient times," he said. "So I did the shamanic journey, and what I saw was I was her only son, and she didn't have husband, and someone was attacking our village, and I somehow died in the fight guarding her. And separate from that I learned that a healer told her she lost her son in the battle many lifetimes back. That's why she's so attached on me. Because she found me after she lost me in the previous lives."

"Or she's in love with you?"

"Or maybe both is true," he said. "I tried to stop it. We did some rituals, we did some ceremonies, but there is still some strange energy happening."

"Don't you ever get tired of people?" I asked.

"That's the service," he said. "I'm trying to motivate others by my strength, which I'm sure I have because of my strong conscious work on having clean connection with my roots. But I'm not the teacher, I'm the one saying, *Hey let's do something and let's learn together.*"

"HOW DOES IT feel to be watching?" someone whispers in my ear. It's a woman I don't recognise.

"I am looking at you and asking how it feels to watch and don't dance," she says. Her eyelids are moving at half speed.

"It's fine," I say.

"I'm sorry," she says. "I wanted to try and connect with you, but now I must seem very strange."

Have I met her before? Does she know I'm with Kuba? Or is she just a random person on mushrooms?

I find Kuba next to his van with a woman. "Where were you, lásko?" he asks.

"Where were *you?*" I don't even look at the woman.

"I was searching for you! I went to move some instruments, and when I came back you were gone."

Whatever. I'm relieved to have found him. I sit next to him.

"I met someone," I say. I don't care if the girl speaks English or not.

"Who was that?" Kuba asks.

"He was leading a ritual. He said you were like Penny Market and he was like Tesco."

Kuba laughs. "Jeroným. Did you tell him I'm actually Globus?"

"No, I like Penny Market."

"He can be the king of Czech esoteric show business," he says. "But I have the most beautiful woman on the world."

When it's time to leave, he vanishes again. I sit in the van and eat dried mango while I wait. When he comes back, another woman intercepts him. I see her in the side mirror—the way she looks at him, the way he touches the flower in her hair. They talk for a while before he brings her over and introduces her to me. When he reaches into my bag of mango and offers her a piece, I want to say, *I'm sick of waiting for you, and that's my fucking mango.*

On the drive home, I say, "I know you like to be with people, but I find it difficult that I spend so much time waiting for you."

"You're right, my love," he says. "Thank you. I don't want to promise you it won't happen again, but I promise you I will do my best."

I've never experienced this kind of communication before. It's better than arguing, I guess, but it's also like hitting a wall. There's nowhere for the emotion to go.

"Do we need to discuss more?" he asks. "Or can we let it go now?"

"We can let it go."

He says, "This is heaven."

"It is," I say. "Once upon a time."

Summer

KUBA SAYS AYAHUASCA showed him that ninety-nine percent of his life is trying to be better than others, and the rest is trying to be obviously humble. "And I was laughing," he says. "Because I saw it all melted down like icebergs into the lake, and I saw my entire life effort is about something what doesn't exist."

We're driving south, stopping to bury or collect dead birds, as usual. My face is inflamed, and my tongue feels weird. Kuba's lifestyle makes it hard for me to maintain my diet and take my supplements, but I'm not complaining. I believe this is what I'm supposed to be doing, even if it's exhausting.

We turn off the road and stop by a shrine. "This is the place where I was sleeping during my teenage years," he says. The shrine is a statue of the Virgin Mary housed in a stone shelter with words written under it. I ask him what it says.

"There is written, because me, the, something like the divine caregiver, am your God, who is holding on your hand and telling you: don't be afraid. I am helping you." When he sees my tears, he hugs me, and alongside the real feelings I'm having I'm aware of my desire to tell him my sad story *with feeling*. I say, "It's what my mother embroidered on a handkerchief for me." Then I have to explain what a handkerchief is, and embroidery, and after that the moment has passed.

We have a picnic next to the shrine so I don't have to discuss my diet with his friends as soon as I meet them. I've found a few foods that work—rice cakes, something called streichcreme, dried mango, fresh fruits and vegetables, this delicious fried tempeh. It's good enough, but I continue to lose weight.

After our picnic, we drive to a farmhouse. Inside, several young people sit around a table drinking and smoking, and a woman on a bed in the corner eats watermelon and spits the seeds onto the floor. Kuba asks if any of them speak English. Someone says no, and they all laugh. A pretty girl sitting close to us pokes Kuba in the belly, and he bends down to hug her. He doesn't introduce me to anyone.

"Don't worry, everyone here is friendly," one of the girls says in English.

I say, "Hi. I'm Mája."

She says, "I know. I know everything about you. Do you eat meat?"

I'm aware the others are listening. I say, "I thought you knew everything about me."

"I guess you don't eat meat and you don't drink alcohol."

"No."

"So here you are fucked," she says, and they all laugh.

Kuba sits at the table between the pretty girl and a guy who's dressed like a medieval serf—belted tunic, hood, and everything. Kuba has a full glass of beer and a bowl of guláš in front of him, and he's smoking. He has his back to me, and there's no more space at the table, so I sit on a filthy armchair in the corner, and a dog sits with me. Everyone is talking loudly and laughing a lot, and Kuba is being rough and loud like the rest of them. No one speaks to me, and eventually even the dog abandons me.

When I was twelve, I went through a mute phase that lasted for about a year. It was like I was trapped in a glass sphere—I could see other people, and they could see me, but there was no way for me to reach out or for anyone else to reach in. The best I could hope for was to be an object of pity, and I didn't want that, so instead I learned to be an observer. Like a spy from another universe, I watched and made my notes. Now I do the same, but the difference is that although I still feel like a reject, I'm not so sure it's my fault.

On the wall there's a crucifix, a picture of a Taliban soldier, and what looks like an ss helmet. There are at least five dogs roaming around, and every surface is covered with stuff. Bridles, saddles, books, metal roses, a wasps' nest, horns, feathers, an antique radio, photographs, paper birds, party hats, tools, knick-knacks.

Even more confusing than this scene itself is how Kuba fits into it. He's clearly not a typical example of someone from his culture, but what even is his culture? He seems to have so many. Last week, we went to a folklore festival in Slovakia. There were up to 100 people on the stage singing and dancing together at a time. It was gorgeous and everything, but there was also something alienating about it. Intimidating, even. Kuba said that's the power of music. It's how the Hussites won wars. "If you heard how unified they were," he said. "And they're singing they are the fighters for the God and the law of the God. If I'm not with them, I'm out of there."

At the festival campground, the music carried on all night. For a while we joined one of the groups playing among the tents. Kuba played koncovka and seemed to know every song. In the middle of the night, a man asked if they could tone it down, and one of them said, "I can hear from your accent that you're from

Prague. You don't tell us what to do here." I don't know why it surprised me. Regional rivalries exist everywhere. One of Kuba's musician friends, who says he's not Czech but Moravian, told me a joke: A man from Prague goes to Brno and asks how he can get to the main station. The answer: "With that accent, with great difficulty."

"Don't you want guláš?" the English-speaking girl says. "It's made from the horse." I say no thanks and space out again while they keep speaking in Czech.

When he's finished his beer, Kuba and I find a place to park for the night. I get ready for bed while he returns a torch to that pretty girl, whose name is Jana. While he's gone, I wipe off my makeup and examine myself in the mirror. Every time I expect it to be different. My skin healed, my tongue normal. I stick out my tongue. It's actually white. I make an ugly face and turn out the light.

Once I'm in my sleeping bag, I realise he's going to take forever, because he always takes forever. I pretend to be sleeping when he comes back. He whispers in my ear, "Jana says she likes you."

"She's rude. They all are."

"She shies to speak English," he says. "But she is good friend." He strokes my belly.

"Why didn't you introduce me to anyone?"

"Actually no one introduced to anyone," he says. "It was strange meeting, and I didn't know how to behave. I think no one did. So they do the jokes and pretend we are all friends and it's cool."

I hadn't thought of that. I was so caught up in myself it didn't occur to me that other people might feel uncomfortable, too.

"Do you ever feel insecure?" I ask.

"Of course!" he says.

"That's hard for me to imagine."

"With that Jeroným, for example."

"Who?"

"Tesco. That guy from the solstice festival. I was afraid you will find him more attractive and successful than me and want to be with him. But I can't follow those feelings, because I would be lost."

I kind of like the idea of him being jealous, but I don't believe it. He strokes my hair. "We are the same," he says. "We have the same insecurities and same fears."

I highly doubt that.

"What is this place?" I ask. "Why do they have all that stuff on the walls, like the ss helmet?"

"The man who owns this house, he's not here today or it would be very different meeting, but he has in his bookshelf a historical ID of the Gestapo and the same he has some historical Soviet Union brigade membership ID. He said, *Look we are always invaded, so I'm ready. They can come from the west, they can come from the east, I'll be ready. I'll have something to show them.*"

"Is that a joke?"

"Isn't it funny?"

"It's sad."

He says, "There is nothing more powerful than my love to you." Then he sings me Kometa, and I fall asleep to the sound of his voice.

HE'S GONE WHEN I wake up, so I stay in the van and watch the news, which is awful, as always. Then I wash my hands with a cup of water and apply concealer to my scars. Inside the house, the woman who was eating watermelon on the bed last night is still in the same place. Kuba and the others are at the table talking loudly. I hear Kuba say Pavla's name.

"Hello," the English-speaking girl says.

I say, "Dobrý den," and she makes an impressed face.

Kuba pulls me onto his lap and kisses my cheek. I ask him what they're talking about. He says that Pavla, his ex-bandmate, speaks excellent English, and she might come in the afternoon. I wish I could have a break from meeting new people. Just for one day.

There's an older man who wasn't here last night. He's talking to Kuba, and I can tell they're talking about me. I understand the words "three passports." Kuba likes to show off that I've been everywhere and nothing impresses me. So do I, if I'm honest, but I'd never be so obvious about it.

"Do we have that rooster?" the man says in English to the woman on the bed. "We have to feed the princess by it."

He's drinking orange soda and spreading something pink onto slabs of meat, which he eats as he talks.

The woman brings a pan of cold chicken and serves it to me. The man continues to speak in Czech as I surreptitiously move the gelatinous meat onto Kuba's plate.

"He's talking about the DNA," Kuba says. "How the messages are stamped there from the aliens. He says the *Bhagavad Gita* says humans only think we are the authors of things."

I think the book I'm reading has something to say about this. Ancient codes hidden in our DNA to . . . I've lost track, honestly. Whenever I try to read it, a mist gathers in my mind.

I wash my plate and go to check my emails in the van using Kuba's cellphone. There's a notification from the genealogy website. I click on the link and sign in. A distant cousin has responded, but it's in Czech. I put it through Google Translate. She says she asked her mother and her aunt, but neither of them had heard of my mother or her family. I write back Děkuji mnohokrát, which Google tells me means thank you very much.

A chat from my father. He asks if I can Skype, which means he's probably depressed.

"Can you hear me?" he says. I can see two of my half-sisters in the background.

"What time is it there?" I ask.

"I thought you'd forgotten who I was," he says.

"How are you doing?"

"I'm cruising along. Although I have no car, because the garage deliberately tried to charge me $5,500 for something that didn't need doing. It was all set up and . . . pianificato?"

"Planned."

"Yes! And I started doing my own investigations under the guidance of a retired engineer . . ." He goes on. I'm not listening. He always has something to rant about. Some fuckwit who screwed him. Some dipshit who he's going to set straight. And he inevitably drops in an Italian word as if he's forgotten the English one.

Even he admits that being famous in his milieu wasn't good for his personality development, but I think living in Thailand also didn't help. He got away with too much. Now that he's back in New Zealand and retired (or no longer working, anyway), he gets no special treatment, and it seems to be softening him. His rants are increasingly peppered with comments so out of character I sometimes wonder if he's losing his mind.

"She doesn't know what she wants to do," he says. He's talking about my oldest half-sister, Mia, who will be graduating high school next year. "I encourage her not to know. Usually you find destiny leads you to it if you put yourself in the right place. But I feel sorry for you kids. Because it's a terrible world at the moment. Somehow it was more kind and gentle fifty years ago."

"You mean it was more gentle and kind to people like you," I say.

"I mean people still believed in things," he says.

This is not the father I grew up with. *Destiny* and *gentle* and *believe* are not words I would ever expect to hear him say, and I also assumed that, like me, my half-sisters would stop being his little darlings as soon as they reached puberty, but even the oldest one, who is extremely unappealing, can still do no wrong in his eyes.

The closest he's come to saying something nice to me since I was eleven was the one time I visited him in Thailand. He'd received an insurance windfall after a Vietnam veteran took exception to him kicking a stray dog at an internet café and bashed him over the head with a stone statue, so instead of trying to drum up funding for his next project he was free to spend his days doting on his new baby and devising ways to kill the monkeys on his balcony.

I was fourteen then, not long out of my mute phase, and still very weird—not quirky or eccentric, weird. I had recently cut off all my hair and eyelashes. Gina tried to get her hairstylist to fix it, but there wasn't much to work with. When my father saw me at the airport, he said, "Hey, Pinocchio!" He explained that it was funny because Pinocchio wished he was a real boy. That pretty much set the tone for the visit. Then one night after dinner with his creepy friends, several of whom tried to get me to sit on their laps, he put his arm around me and said, "Seriously though, love. You have a good face and body. You should do more with yourself."

"This year Lucia has one teacher I'd like to clock one," he says, talking about another daughter now. "But I sorted her out. Poor little sausage forgot her bathers, and the teacher made her stay after school and write *I must remember to bring my togs* on the board one hundred times. I went in there and said, *This is no longer the 1950s. That will not happen again, understand?* She got the message loud and clear. I certainly sorted her out. And the principal. God, he's a scummy, uptight prick. Awful person. He's even got a Union Jack tattooed on him. Just a total loser. So I can tell I'm going to have more battles with him."

As usual, I'm left feeling sorry for my father's girlfriend, who's only eight years older than me, and for my half-sisters with Italian names, one of which is almost exactly the same as mine, in case I had any doubts about whether I'd been replaced.

BACK AT THE house, Kuba is sitting on the porch with Pavla. I wouldn't have recognised her from Facebook. She looks sporty and severe. Her hair, which was long and brown in all the photos I've seen, is dyed black with chunky purplish highlights and cut in an asymmetrical bob. She shakes my hand. There's no long hug, no staring. After a brief silence, she says, "I feel shy," and goes inside.

I sit on Kuba's lap and take the cigarette from between his fingers. I ask him if he and Pavla were ever more than friends.

"Impossible," he says.

"Why?"

"Well, in past she was married, and she has a child," he says. "But also it was necessary to keep a clean space between us, because it was powerful what we were creating together, so we consciously decided not to mess it up by sex."

She comes back onto the porch. "You're smoking?" she says. I don't know why that would surprise her.

She wants to make a fire, so I offer to help. As we collect kindling, she asks a constant stream of questions. *Do you want a family? How does your ex-boyfriend feel about you leaving him? What do you think about Otto? Do you like living in his house?* I find her directness charming and even relaxing after being around so many people I can't read.

"How do you like Kubík's mother?" she asks.

"She seems nice," I say. "I've only met her once, and she doesn't speak English, so . . ."

"Do you want to live in the Czech Republic?"

"I don't think so."

"Isn't it a problem?"

"Yes."

"Kubík loves to travel, but he is a Czech man."

"I noticed."

"What does your family think about him?"

"They only know the general idea."

"And what is the general idea?"

"I guess that he's very spiritual? I was missing that in my past relationship."

"And do you like it now?"

"It's challenging sometimes, to be honest, but there are definitely aspects that I like."

"I hear you like our folk music," she says.

He must talk about me a lot.

"I do," I say. "I actually don't really know how much of the music I like is technically folk music."

"How do you understand it?" she asks.

"Folk music? In English we use the same name for music like Nohavica, but I assume that's not folk like folk. Kuba told me that Czech folk music has different characteristics in different regions, but I don't know if that's true about all folk music or . . ."

"That's a very romantic idea," she says. "Maybe it's true to a point, because Communists misused folk culture as propaganda, and of course every village wanted to distinguish itself from the neighbouring village. But as a musician, it's natural that Kuba has romantic beliefs about such things."

"Aren't the romantic ideas of folk musicians also part of the folk . . ."

"Tradition?" she says. "Sorry, I can't use that word without quotation marks, because what does it mean? People made some music before, people make some music now. Is it less authentic now?"

"So is there anything definitive you would say about Czech folk music?" I ask.

"Yes," she says. "I like it."

"Me too," I say.

"You know you are very special to Kubík," she says. "He has a lot of opportunities to have relationships, but he told me you are the person who he has been waiting for his whole life."

I ask her about herself. She says her new boyfriend is a computer programmer named Adam, she's not interested in spiritual men, and she doesn't make music any more. Last year she opened a health food store.

WHEN THE FIRE is going, we return to the farmhouse. Kuba is on the porch. I sit on his lap. We can hear the others inside.

"I'm leaving," Pavla says.

"Why?" I ask.

"I feel a big block," she says. "Because everyone in there has a conflict between what they feel inside and what they show." That's what I've felt most of my life, but I've never heard anyone say it.

Kuba is kissing my shoulder. Pavla shines her flashlight on us. "It's nice to see you together," she says. "But it makes me miss my Adámek. So, I just came to make a fire with you." She picks up her backpack and walks off down the driveway.

"Is she really leaving?" I ask.

Kuba says, "She is so strange person."

"I like her."

"I also do," he says.

At the fire, Kuba and the others sing loud songs while I watch the flames. Slowly, everyone gets quieter, and then Kuba sings Kometa, and they all sing with him.

I SKIPPED HIS drum-making workshop so I could have time to recover before the Czech dance camp. Instead, I've been spending all my time Googling my symptoms. I look at forums, read hundreds of anecdotes and journal articles, trying to find something helpful, and eventually giving up. I'm a sickly person with bad skin, inflammation, a weird tongue thing, and hypnopompic hallucinations (at least I learned a fancy word in my searching).

I told Kuba about the shaking walls. I wondered if there might be a connection with the reason he shakes. He said, "You probably had an experience in the dream that as part of the recovery you have the feeling of the false shaking."

"So it's in my head?"

"I think I would notice if the walls were shaking."

I hadn't expected him to be so matter-of-fact about it. When I told Gina, she said I need to take magnesium and get a ceramic water filter, because it's caused by fluoride.

A friend of Otto's has moved into the garden. Her name is Sophie. She says Otto doesn't hate women, but he's had some bad experiences. She has vertigo and can't fly, so when she wants to go on a holiday she hitchhikes here from her cottage in the mountains and spends her time cooking over the fire and putting dried flower petals into small muslin bags. She calls it "flower petal love magic."

I sit with her in the evening, and she offers me a baked potato. I ask her what it's like to have vertigo. She says, "It's like falling down inside yourself," which is a wonderful description and something I'll have to write down.

I ask her how her magic works. She says, "I pick flowers, and a word comes into my head of what they are for. Like forgiveness, unconditional understanding, trust. And when I'm drying them that intention has gone into them, and they forever mean that. Then I put them in a little bag all together for someone to be with them to help them get through what they're going through."

I decide to tell her about the shaking walls. She cuts the white flesh of her potato into cubes with a pocket knife as she listens.

"Spirits," she says.

"Oh yeah?"

"Those are messengers from the other side."

"What do they want?"

"I don't know," she says. "Did you ask them?"

"No. I just wait for it to be over."

"It's normal for the body to react when you start to be interested in spiritual things," she says. "Like with my vertigo. It's a messenger. I ask it what it wants."

"What does it want?"

"It wants me to keep my feet on the ground."

I miss Kuba so much, but it's healthy to have a break. I can think more clearly, and there's time to Skype with people from home, although no one understands what I'm doing. When I tell Becca about how ayahuasca helped Kuba to see through his inner structures, she says her mildew cleaner does that for her. We haven't Skyped in over a month because of the time difference and Kuba's erratic schedule, and now that we are talking, I only feel more distant from her, as if we were living on different planets.

WE'RE SUPPOSED TO have two days at home before the dance camp, but he comes home a day late, and there's some issue with the marquee, so when he gets back from his workshop we have to leave immediately.

While we're packing, he says, "Oh, love, I need to know one thing. I don't want to put a pressure, but will you go to India with me? The tickets are coming to be more and more expensive."

I tell him I can't afford it, and he says, "Say yes and I will buy you the ticket now."

"What would that mean?"

"I lost all my visions," he says. "I got the email from the place where I wanted to put our bus saying it's not legal for me to park there."

"Why?"

"It's my fault," he says. "One of the owl wings was wounded, so I kept only a few feathers for myself, but I loved the other wing so much I didn't want to give it to those people, and that's why it doesn't work."

"So?"

"So we have to go there, to bring the wing and everything else from the bird and offer it to the place."

"Okay, but if it works, what would it mean if I don't want to live there?"

"I'm not afraid," he says.

"But we're just making more pain for ourselves."

"Why to live at all then?" he says. "If we know it's painful and we will die, why not stop it now? Because I love you, and I came here to learn."

"Can you really imagine having children with me?" I ask.

"I'm imagining it since first time I saw you."

"But don't you see it's impossible if we can't agree on where to live?"

"We would have to change a lot of things, but I'm ready for that. I want to live on one place and make the stable family life."

"Do you really think you can do that?"

"Are you asking me if I'm too selfish for being suitable with family life?"

"No. I don't think you're selfish."

"I am," he says. "Almost everyone is selfish, and I am also selfish."

"And I'm a shellfish," I say.

He puts his hand over my heart and groans. "If I start to think you might leave me, I have to hold it, because if I go into the feelings, I will cry one week. Please don't talk about leaving me ever."

I tell him I won't, but we both know it's not that simple. I have to make some decisions about my life before it's too late. I'm running out of money, and when that happens, I'll run out of options, end up like my father, or worse, like my mother—displaced, friendless, sick, bitter, like The Lady of Shalott destroying herself for a man only to have him coolly observe her stony dead body and say, "She has a lovely face."

"I have something for you," he says. He looks through his backpack and pulls out an envelope. "From the matrix."

He lets me open it, then he reads. "It is written there that Jan Svoboda, your uncle?"

"Yes."

"Born 17/09/1957 in České Budějovice, died 21/04/1966 because of the, um, trauma . . ." he touches his head.

"Traumatic head injury."

"Yes. Location of death, České Budějovice."

"Okay."

"And Miloš Svoboda, so that's your grandfather, died 12/06/1972 for, um, cirhózu?"

"Cirrhosis."

"Of the . . ."

"Liver."

"Yes. Location of death, České Budějovice."

"Okay."

"So it means he was not born on České Budějovice, because they do not record his birth."

"Okay."

"And your grandmother, Marie Svobodová, born 29/01/1937 on České Budějovice, died 08/09/2008, in age of seventy-one years."

"Of?"

"They say they stop to include that information in records before she died, but she definitely died on České Budějovice, because they have her death recorded there."

2008 was the year I finished grad school. Drew and I spent the summer in Greece. We rode our bikes to ruins and beaches, and I carried sesame snaps in my bag for the fettered animals. If I'd known my grandmother was alive then, would I have tried to meet her? I was finally happy. Why would I want to find some miserable old woman who had never bothered to find me?

"Is that all?" I ask.

"Your mother. Dorota Svobodová, born 12/04/1961 in České Budějovice. No further records."

THE CAMP IS at a retreat centre with a normal bathroom, plumbing, and hot water. We have a private room with a desk and a door that locks. I was so relieved when I saw it I almost cried.

He's outside helping to erect the marquee. I've just woken up from a nightmare. I don't remember what happened, but there's this feeling of threat and losing something important, and now the walls are shaking, and I feel wretched.

I'm wearing the white dress I bought to wear to the opening ceremony. I don't think I can go out there in it, though. I'm not sure I can go out there at all. I look out the window. There are already so many people. I recognise Kuba's mother, Pavla, Véra, the woman from the frog thing, Marie, the woman from the dances in České Budějovice, Barbora, Kuba's past-life mother, and Šárka, the woman from the dances in the forest.

I wonder if the other Mája is here. I've searched his Facebook friends for women with various versions of my name, but I didn't find any likely candidates. I did find that České Budějovice Marie. In her profile picture, she's mostly naked in a field of wheat with her head thrown back, playing a frame drum.

I change into loose drawstring pants and a T-shirt, and Kuba and I walk to the opening ceremony together. There's a birch branch archway on the lawn in front of the marquee. Four women wearing brightly-coloured dresses and flower crowns are standing in front of it with baskets of bread and plates of salt.

Véra comes up beside me and puts her arm around my waist. Kuba and two other men play large, intricately-carved wooden flutes, and people start to gather. Everyone seems to know what to do. Once a group has formed, Kuba puts down his flute, picks up his guitar, and sings something. People repeat the words. "It means welcome in the circle," Véra says.

The call and response continues as people queue up to take bread and salt from the women with the baskets and walk through the arch. "This one is gluten free," Véra says, taking my hand and moving me toward one of the women. We both take bread, dip it in salt, and eat it. Then we walk through the arch together.

Before we enter the marquee, someone takes my other hand, and like at the New Zealand camp, we make a snake and walk around looking into each other's eyes and repeating what Kuba is singing. "We celebrate the earth," Véra translates. "We celebrate the roots. We celebrate life, connected to everything. We celebrate water, the natural flow. We celebrate fire, charged by the energy. We celebrate the wind, in each our breath. Welcome in the circle, connected with the spirit."

Once everyone is inside, we make one big circle, and Kuba finds me and stands next to me. "Welcome in the family," he sings in English, and he squeezes my hand.

In the silence after the song, Kuba's mother pushes in between us and rubs her nose against my shoulder. They say their opening prayer in various languages, and I look around at all the faces. Pavla, Véra, Šárka, Kuba's mother, the children lying in a heap on blankets in the middle. I wish I could relax and enjoy this. Turn off the voice that keeps telling me I'm not welcome. I don't belong.

HE'S SO BUSY I've hardly seen him since we got here, but I've met many of his friends, or whatever these people are to him. "Oh, you're so lucky!" one woman says. "He is the shooting star in the dance world! He is so special to everyone! People love him! And he's so young! And so humble! To do dances with him is something very special!"

Véra's ex-partner Tadeáš, who is also a dance leader, is here with his girlfriend. He's older than Kuba and very tall with long, blonde hair. When we meet, he puts his hands on my waist and calls me "my little girl," which I find gross but also pleasant, because understanding that my relationship with my father makes me tolerant of a certain kind of treatment from a certain kind of man doesn't make me any less tolerant of it.

At lunch, I sit next to Pavla and her boyfriend. She scoffs at my plate, which only has salad on it. I could tell her that we have to do a strict diet to prepare for ayahuasca, but I don't need to explain myself.

I ask how they're enjoying the camp. She turns to her boyfriend and says, "What did she say?" then continues to talk to him in Czech as if I wasn't there. I can't understand why she's being so rude to me.

Back in our room, I open Facebook and check her profile. Apart from the profile picture, almost *every* picture has Kuba in it, and there isn't one picture of her and her boyfriend.

I look out the window. Kuba is in the field talking to two women. I can only see their skirts, because they're behind a tree. He reaches into his pocket and gives them each something. Crystals, I guess.

I'M READING ABOUT the commodification of ayahuasca. Apparently Walmart sells smudge sticks. Crystals are becoming the new blood diamonds. I hear Kuba on the stairs. I already know the sound of his footfall. He said he would have dinner with me, but he didn't show up. I get out of bed and sit at my computer so I can pretend I was working.

"I have to do an interview," he says. "A documentary filmmaker came."

He leaves, and I resolve that whatever happens, when he comes back I will ignore him. At two a.m. he wakes me up by touching me. I push his hands away.

"Where were you?" I ask.

"I'm so tired," he says.

"I thought we were going to spend time together." I have to pee, but I'm afraid if I get up, he'll leave.

"Here I am," he says.

"Why are you always giving people crystals?" I ask. I had planned to bring it up in a joking way. Instead it comes out whiny and accusatory.

"It's a big treasure to our friends, because I was bringing my bag full of crystals and keeping it overnight by the grave of my teacher in India."

It's sad to imagine the souls of dead people waiting around for human beings to want things from them. "Why does that make it a treasure?"

"I felt transmission there," he says.

The first time I heard him use this word, I thought it was one of his many cute malapropisms, but now I know it's part of dance leader lingo. Whenever there's more than one dance leader around, the conversation turns to leading—who will lead, what they will lead, where it came from, how they will lead it, and who does and doesn't have transmission, which is important because the dances are meant to be received, not invented. Kuba, of course, has transmission out the wazoo.

"Why do you only give them to your women friends?"

He strokes my hair. "I know it's not easy that I have so many women friendships," he says. "But freedom is about trust and responsibility, and if I don't trust you, it means I don't think you are responsible."

He lies down with his head on my chest. "You can totally relax, lásko," he says. "Like I told you, if you think that after what we have experienced together I can be thinking about other woman, you really are dummy."

I'M TRYING TO go to the marquee as much as possible, but it's so hard, and it keeps getting harder. When I do go out and talk to people, they're almost always nice, but I'm so over the touching and eye contact, and I can't shake the feeling that I'm being watched. I'm also fed up with the simplistic, aggressively positive takes on world religions, and how they talk about *the outside world* as if it's this homogenous, bad thing and they are the good society.

The dances I find mostly boring, sometimes funny, sometimes excruciating, and occasionally deeply moving. There was one about the women in Jesus' life. The woman who led it said it was about connecting with female ancestors. Only the women danced it. I've never been into the idea of sisterhood or goddess circles, but as I looked around at the other women dancing, I told myself that I could get a lot out of this experience if I could see them not as soul sisters, but as friends.

Many of them have tried. Often someone sits with me and initiates a chat, hugs me, translates for me. Claire, one of the camp organisers, speaks French. She gave me a sachet of lavender to put under my pillow. I appreciate these gestures, but I always wonder if they're being nice to me because of my proximity to someone special, which is probably just another hangup from my life with my father. Afterwards, back in our room, I feel exposed and embarrassed. If I've been myself, I'm sure they'll think I'm strange, or a snob, and if I haven't, I feel like a fraud remembering how I used their words, *intention* and *heart sharing*, how I gazed into Claire's eyes as if I was bathing in open-hearted presence when really I was just waiting for it to be over.

People also keep commenting on the fact that I'm in the marquee less and less, which fuels my paranoia about being watched. One woman said, "It's great to see you out, Mája," as if I'm a vampire.

In the lunch queue, a man I've never seen before said, "Mája, you are an ice queen." I asked if he knew what it meant. He said,

"You are almost never smiling. I mean right now you are, but usually not."

It's not the first time I've been told to *smile, pretty girl.*

"Do you feel lonely?" he asked.

I said, "Sometimes I miss my friends."

"You are very brave," he said. When people describe my writing that way I take it to mean ill-considered, unwise.

"How about you?" I asked. "Are you lonely?"

He said, "Here I am not lonely. I'm in my head a lot in my work, and dances help me to connect with my body and heart, so that is helping me."

"That's great," I said. "I'm glad it helps."

I'M WATCHING AN interview with a French doctor named Jacques Mabit, who went to Peru to establish a health centre for Médecins Sans Frontières in 1980, when he was twenty-five. After seeing the effectiveness of the methods and techniques used by the traditional healers he encountered, he later returned to the country to train with Amazonian curanderos, specialists in traditional medicine, including the ritual application of ayahuasca and other "teacher plants."

"They told me *do that, do that,* and I did it, even if I didn't understand," he says. "Because if I started to analyse it rationally, I wouldn't have done it . . . When I asked how the plants work, they responded with very poor sentences from a western rationalist perspective. I would say, *How do the plants teach?* And they would say, *They teach by teaching.* I would say, *Why do they heal?* And they would say, *Because they have healing properties.* And each time I accepted that it's not through words, but through experience with the plants, because the plant could speak to you."

He says the first time he drank ayahuasca, nothing happened. "I was very scared, very on the defensive, and I blocked everything," he says. The second time, he immediately found himself being dragged into an abyss by a boa constrictor. "It was a terrible experience," he says. "Externally I stayed very calm. I realised afterward that everything happened inside, in my depths. I resisted death, I gathered all my resources, but the snake was stronger than me. There was nothing I could do, and I was angry with myself. I was thinking, why did I take this drug? This is something for Indigenous people, not for whites, and now I'm dying. I was thinking how my parents will say, *Our son was a doctor, he went to Amazonia, and he took a drug, and he died.* I saw myself dead in a coffin, everything that could happen as a consequence, and bit by bit, acceptance. Because there was nothing I could do. I couldn't call the healer or cry. I was totally trapped."

He says he accepted that his life had been what it had been, and in the morning the world would carry on without him. "I realised I wasn't important. And at that moment, a sentence came to me, but it was like it came from outside, and it was *Jacques is not important. Jacques is not important. Jacques is not important.* Three times. And the third time, when I accepted that I had no importance, the snake disappeared, and there I was in this abyss, but at that moment, I let go."

The eighth time he drank ayahuasca, he says he was confronted by a panel of beings who introduced themselves as the guardian spirits of the jungle and asked him why he was there. He said that he wanted to learn to work with the medicine, and they told him that he had permission, but his path would be to treat people with addictions. He had no interest or experience in that field, so he dismissed the message and continued his apprenticeship with traditional healers.

Three years later, he had an ayahuasca session where a woman asked him if he was sincere about wanting to work with plants. He confirmed that he was, and she said that he should remember his assignment. He agreed.

The next morning, a psychiatrist from Lima called Mabit and and his wife, Peruvian physician Dr. Rosa Giove Nakazawa, who was also immersed in learning about traditional medicine, especially from women healers and midwives. The psychiatrist asked Mabit and Giove if they would accept a patient with a substance use disorder. They accepted the referral, and that was the beginning of Takiwasi, the non-profit rehabilitation centre and therapeutic community they co-founded in 1992, where psychotherapy is integrated with traditional Amazonian medicine in a nine-month residential programme.

I click on a link to another interview. In this one, Mabit is talking about the mythical horizons that predominate in different epochs, with tribal societies being governed by what he calls the myth of Justice, where reciprocity is emphasised and the group takes precedence over the individual, and westernised societies being governed by what he calls the myth of Love, which centres the individual and emphasises forgiveness.

I'm so interested in what he's saying, but just as he's about to introduce the myth that he believes is emerging now, the video ends. I try to find another version, but I can't.

KUBA IS TALKING to Pavla outside the marquee. I sit next to him, and he puts his arm around me. "How are you, lásko?" he says. "I was sad I didn't see you at dances this morning."

I start to answer him, but Pavla interrupts me to say something in Czech, which seems a bit rude since it's just the three of us. She points at a shirtless man practicing qigong in the field.

"Don't do that," Kuba says.

"What?" she says. "I just want to know if he has a girlfriend."

"Don't you have a boyfriend?" he asks.

Pavla says, "You have *her*, but you're still open." It takes a second for me to understand that she's talking about me. Kuba pulls me closer but doesn't say anything.

"You should go and speak to Adámek," she says to me. "He needs to have pretty things around him."

I walk away. I expect Kuba to follow me, but he doesn't. Later, he comes and asks if I would like to have tea and some songs with him under the cherry tree.

"Didn't you find it kind of fucked up that Pavla said you were open to other women?"

"I learned long time ago to ignore her," he says.

"Why would she say that?"

He sits next to me. "Lásko," he says. "She is true that before I was open to attention from many women. Before I met you, I was waiting for you, but I wasn't doing a good job, because the physical body was hungry."

"Do you keep in contact with the women you didn't do a good job with?"

"Few."

"Have I met any of them?"

"Only Marie, but she is like a sister for me."

"*Another* Marie?"

"There is only one apart from you, and that other one what I was thinking about only."

"I'm confused. So there's the one you met in a tea room who looks like me and who you thought you might want to be with and another one you slept with?"

"Yes."

"And do you see the one you slept with?"

"Of course."

"Why haven't you introduced me to her?"

"I did," he says. "She's here."

"What?"

"Marie," he says. "From Plseň. You met her on the dances on České Budějovice."

"Are you serious?"

"I told you about it at the restaurant after dances, and you were bit upset."

"You did not."

"I did."

"You don't think I would remember that?"

"You were upset, you remember? You were also jealous about Véra."

"I was *not* jealous about Véra!" I know I wasn't. Was I?

"My love," he says. "My dream is to make you feel safe and happy."

"This is hard," I say. "There's so much I don't understand."

"I'm imagining it all the time," he says. "You are so brave."

"I need to know what's going on, okay?"

"Of course," he says.

"And Pavla is an asshole."

"Yes."

SHAKING WALLS AGAIN. I woke up drenched in sweat and so anxious. Today is my birthday. Kuba said he would skip the afternoon session so we could spend some time together, but he had to meditate for twenty minutes first. That was three hours ago.

I get up, wash my face, and reapply my makeup before going outside. I find him sitting with two women, including Marie. He says, "Excuse me, lásko." I ignore him and go back to our room.

People keep telling me how lucky I am, but at the moment I don't feel lucky. I feel unwell and exhausted and increasingly angry. There must be a lesson in all of this, but I'm too upset to figure out what it is, and I'm starting to think that it can fuck off.

I open my computer and type, "Help, my boyfriend is a shaman" into Google. Nothing helpful. At least it makes me smile.

When Kuba comes back, he has excuses, as usual. Some friend was leaving and he had to say goodbye, those women are his students and they had some questions for him. All he had to do was to tell me those things were more of a priority than our plans. It would have taken two minutes, and then I wouldn't have been waiting for *three hours* for him to show up.

He says, "Can you come and lie down with me?"

"I have to work," I say, although that's ludicrous because I'm not in any frame of mind to work and haven't been for a long time.

He comes over to where I'm sitting and pulls my chin up so I'm looking at him. Who am I kidding? He can do whatever he wants with me, and he knows it.

He reaches into his back pocket and takes out a small paper bag. Inside is a fine silver chain with a rectangular pendant embossed with an image of a woman in a flowing gown holding her arms up and looking toward the sky. She wears a flower crown and carries a cornucopia in one hand and what looks like yarn in the other. Her lower body seems to extend into the earth like roots.

"She is Mokoš," he says. "The Slavic mother goddess. She represents the life force, the destiny, the fruitality."

"Fertility," I say. I'm not really into jewellery, but I'll wear it for now. He helps me to put it on, then assesses me.

"Ty jsi tak božská žena," he says. "Just a goddess."

He sits on the bed. "How are you, lásko?" he asks.

"Honestly?"

"Of course."

"I feel uncomfortable."

"Why?"

"Many reasons."

"Can you share them with me?"

"I think I'm just not a joiner. I feel uncomfortable in groups where everybody agrees with each other."

"If you come to team meeting you will pretty soon see that we don't all agree," he says.

"I'm just saying that there are kind of unspoken . . . like how you divide things into men and women, and the way that different religions . . . it's like you make them fit a version of reality that you all seem to agree on, but it's not necessarily how they're meant, you know?"

"I'm not leading the dances where I don't have personal relationship to the tradition what it comes from," he says. "And the dance leaders and people who bring the dances come from many different cultures and traditions also. But you are true that some people are like magpies collecting whatever and start to teach it after hearing one time without understanding at all."

"Does that bother you?"

"Sometimes," he says. "But what I'm sure about is that whatever someone does, he is getting perfect feedback."

"From who?"

"From life."

"And what feedback are you getting?"

"It's different," he says. "Sometimes support. Sometimes the strong slap. I'm learning all the time. But what I believe is it's about the relationship, and also the relationship with own roots, so you know where you are coming from and you have something to share. But in my travels, and here in Czech Republic, I met elders from many different traditions, and what I got from all of them is that we are supposed to help each other and learn from each other, because we are here for such a little moment, and we're so consumed by our mind constructs that we don't know how to care for the planet because we don't know the planet. We don't know how to care for each other because we don't know each other."

I start to tell him about Mabit and the video with no ending, but he looks at his watch and says, "Sorry, love, I have to go. Can you find me and take me to bed after tonight's session?"

I won't be doing that. If he wants to be with me, he knows where to find me, and if he wants to spend five hours hugging people, that's up to him.

TADEÁŠ KNOCKS ON the door. I let him in, and he hugs me like a giraffe drinking water, spreading his legs and pulling me into him.

He says, "I need to connect with you, beloved one," as if we were dear old friends instead of people who met for two minutes a few days ago. He sits on the bed and props his chin on his hand. I sit at the desk. "How *are* you?" he asks.

"Good."

"It must be difficult for you, to be alone so much." How does he know I'm alone? Don't these people have anything better to do?

"I actually like being alone," I say. That used to be true. Now I'm not so sure.

"It was hard for my ex-partner, too," he says. "When I was busy in the middle of the circle, Véra felt bad that I didn't pay attention to her."

Or maybe she felt bad that you were cheating on her.

"But you and Kuba," he says. "You have to think of it like you have a garden, and if you are secure in that garden, you won't mind other people around who would like to be in your place, and if Kuba sees that you don't mind, and if he sees that you take care of your garden, he will know you are a warrior woman."

"Yep," I say. I have no interest in arguing with him.

When he hugs me goodbye, he fingers the sections of my spine.

I sit on the bed. I can hear Kuba singing over everyone else in the marquee. He's out there being adored, waking up every morning and rolling into the circle of love while I'm trapped in here with my unwanted thoughts, including this one: I'm jealous. I wouldn't want all those people hanging off me, but I wish I had a mission and believed in things and knew what to do and say like he does. And I wish I'd had a childhood rich with traditions and warmth and community, not the disjointed randomness of my own upbringing. I hate jealousy, but I am jealous. Not of those women, of Kuba.

TONIGHT THERE'S GOING to be a constellation for Kuba and Barbora, his past-life mother. He says she asked for me to be there, and I've agreed purely out of curiosity.

At lunch, Kuba comes with a plate for me, but there's nothing on it that I can eat except lettuce and a few pieces of cucumber.

"What about our diet?" I ask. We were sent a long list of things we're not supposed to eat before ayahuasca.

"Oh right," he says. "I will start tomorrow."

I take a bite of a soggy leaf.

"You are eating from the unity," he says. The word *jednota* is written in brown letters around the edge of my plate. "During the communism the most common chain of grocery store was called that way, so it's funny that people have such a historical plates on dance camps where everything is about unity, because there was unity everywhere during the totalitarianism."

When he opens the door to leave, Pavla is waiting on the other side. How long has she been there? "Can I speak with you?" she asks.

I invite her in. She sits on the bed.

"My boyfriend left," she says.

"Sorry," I say.

"I was sleeping outside last night," she continues. "And I was hugging myself and feeling like I am a strong woman. You know, I knew it would hurt a lot when I stopped to cooperate with Kubík, because my identity was very connected with him."

"Oh yeah?"

"How is it now, with you and his mother?" she asks.

"Fine. Why?" She asked me that the first time we met.

"Kubík knows exactly what women need to hear," she says. "His woman side is very strong."

I can't tell if she's trying to be friends or what, but my hunch is that she's staking her claim, because she knows all about Kuba, and I'm just learning.

"It can be difficult for you," she says. "So many women love him. But don't worry. It's different with you. You're from another country. That's your plus."

Wow. Thanks.

"Do you miss being in the band with him?" I ask.

"No," she says. "I only wish I had ended it sooner."

I thought he ended it, but I don't say so.

She's crying. I ask if she and her boyfriend broke up.

"He lied to me the whole time!" she says. "And I believed him. Isn't that stupid? I believed that he loved me, and he was the one, but he didn't even believe in ones! I feel so bad. I feel so, so bad."

She keeps crying, and I wait. I never know what to do. "I'm sorry you feel bad," I say.

"My heart is so *fucking* big," she says. "It just takes in everything and everyone, and it hurts so much." She wipes her eyes. "Okay, enough, enough."

She stands up. Before she leaves, she says, "You won't tell Kubík what I said." It's not a question.

WHEN HE COMES back, he asks what Pavla said. Instead of answering, I tell him my worries about my health. He says I should do a shamanic journey, and when he does that he finds his guide, a cow, and he sees the answers in its eyes. That makes me feel very alone.

He convinces me to go to the evening dances, because the constellation with Barbora is immediately afterwards. The dance session is led by Doug and Shanti, an older couple from Canada who are apparently superstars in the dance world. When it's Kuba's turn to lead, he asks everyone to say things that have come up for them at camp that need healing. Pavla is lying on a blanket in the middle of the circle. I feel sorry for her. She seems very lost. Tadeáš says, "Come on, let's dance and dance and dance." I think he expects everyone to laugh, but no one does. People call out words, and Kuba calls out their translations. Envy, insecurity, pretending, manipulation, anger, comparing, sadness, grief. Then we do a dance, and for a while I feel like I love everyone in there, and I feel loved, too. Not safe, but loved.

AFTER THE USUAL hugging following the session, Kuba asks everyone to leave except for the people involved in the constellation—me, Kuba, his mother, Barbora, Shanti, Tadeáš's girlfriend Solstice, two other women, some men, and a woman named Olga, who seems to be the leader.

Barbora is dressed in a white linen gown. We separate into men and women. Solstice offers to translate for me and Shanti, and Olga says that's fine as long as it doesn't interrupt the process.

"Olga is explaining that Kuba and Barbora have been together in a past life," Solstice says. "She was his mother, and he died." Barbora starts to cry, and the other women comfort her. Kuba's mother is rubbing her back. She must be used to this kind of thing.

"She says Barbora and Kuba tried to fix this," Solstice says. "But nothing has worked, and now they want to do this constellation where Kuba will be with her as her son, and then he will turn from her and walk to the men's side."

Barbora is speaking now. "She says they were also lovers in another past life," Solstice says. "It was a secret, and they were separated. So twice she has been separated from him forever."

The other women hold their hands on Barbora's back, but I don't want to touch her. Kuba kneels and does something I can't see by her feet. Then he stands up and turns away from her, and she holds him from behind. She tries to keep hold of him when he pulls away to move toward the men. He seems to be struggling, but finally he breaks free, and she collapses. The other women kneel next to her and stroke her as she wails.

I don't believe in this at all, not because I don't believe in past lives or invisible entities, but because I don't believe Barbora. My only question is, does she believe herself?

Kuba faces the women with the men at his back. Barbora is still weeping on the ground. The flaps at the entrance are held open. Would anyone notice if I left? The women help Barbora up, and when she's standing, Olga stands behind her whispering in her ear.

"She is supposed to repeat what Olga is saying to her," Solstice says.

Barbora tries to speak, but she's crying too much and has to keep starting over. I feel nauseated, and there's a hollow feeling in my throat. Kuba watches from a distance with the men holding their hands on his back.

When Barbora has managed to say whatever Olga is telling her, Kuba and the other men walk in a circle around the inside of the marquee and leave. Once they're gone, the women walk the same circle with Barbora, but we stop by the open flaps. Just when I think it's over and we can go to bed, the men come back in, and Tadeáš stands in front of Barbora.

"He is representing death," Solstice says. "She has to tell to him, *I accept you.*" Barbora starts crying again, and a vile vomit burp burns up my throat. I swallow it.

Barbora manages to get out her sentence, then she falls onto the ground again. Kuba's mother rubs my back. I need to get out of here.

It takes a long time for Barbora to stand up. Meanwhile, the men have gone to bed. The women walk outside and hold hands in a circle. I'm freezing, but the fresh air feels good. Very, very slowly, Barbora goes around the circle and hugs each of the women. When she gets to me, she stares into my eyes for a long time. Her irises are totally black in the darkness. I can't imagine what's happening behind them. Maybe she's trying to forgive me for my lavish good fortune. Maybe she's wishing I would disappear. She hugs me, and when she lets go, she stands at a distance from the rest of the circle and bends forward. I'm not sure if she's bowing or falling over, but the other women bow, so I do, too. She stays bowing for a while, then she stands up and whispers, "Dobrou noc." Finally free, I run away across the field.

KUBA SAYS HE has to get his guitar from the marquee. He insists he will be right back. He isn't. I'm half asleep when he gently shakes me and says, "Lásko, I need your help."

"What is it?"

"One woman is upset. Will you come and hug her?"

I follow him downstairs. Solstice is sitting on the bottom step. She looks fine. Kuba walks away, she follows him, and I follow her. No one says anything. He goes to a grassy area, puts down a blanket, and when he kneels on it, she falls on him and starts weeping. I don't know what to do. I kneel next to them. He's holding her and stroking her hair. Then she gasps, her body goes rigid, and she stares dead-eyed at his chest and speaks in a child's voice.

He's looking at me helplessly. What does he expect me to do? And where the fuck is Tadeáš? She's crying again and gripping Kuba's neck. I look up at the moon and remember the oppressive feeling I used to have when my mother was in pain. There was nothing I could do to help her, but I couldn't carry on as normal.

Fuck this. I don't have to do this. I get up and walk away.

Shanti stops me in the courtyard. "Is it about Solstice?" she asks. "She was upset. She was communicating with the fourth dimension, and we were trying to . . ."

"What the fuck is the fourth dimension? Time?" I'm shaking.

"We did some grounding work, and after she seemed to be okay," she says, backing away slightly. "We couldn't find Tadeáš, so we decided that we should let her go to bed and have someone check her in the morning, and we were asking who should do it, and then Kuba came into the marquee, and . . ."

Of course. Their knight.

"Are you okay?" she asks.

I'm not. I feel like screaming, hitting myself, running away. I don't want to lose control. I hear him behind me. He tries to take my arm, but I pull away and leave him with Shanti.

By the time he comes to bed, I've managed to calm myself down. "Why did you tell me she needed a hug?" I say.

"It's not my mistake," he says. "They left me there with her. I went to get my guitar, and as soon I walked in the marquee she was running to me and holding me and crying, and I asked what's wrong and she said they are gossiping about her and they don't understand her. Then they left me there without telling me nothing, and I didn't know what to do, so I came for you because I thought you would help me. I didn't know why you are standing there and don't hug her."

"Because I don't *want* to hug her! And how were you supposed to help? You're a *musician!*"

He gets into bed next to me. I feel furious and violated, but there's also this thought that sails over the riot of emotions I don't understand: *I'm right.*

ANOTHER SOMETHING-IS-COMING dream. Trying to lock doors and windows, but they were all broken. Same old same old.

There's going to be a final dance session before the marquee comes down. I tell Kuba I'll see him there. When I'm chopping fruit for breakfast Solstice asks if she can speak with me. "I wanted to tell you I had a vision," she says.

"Okay," I say.

She holds her hands up, palms facing each other, fingers spread, then moves them together and interlaces her fingers in front of her face. She's watching me, waiting for me to react.

"I don't understand," I say.

She says, "Oh," and a tear falls down her cheek. "I thought you would understand me."

"I'm sorry," I say. I truly am. I know how painful it is to be misunderstood.

Claire is one of the camp organisers and some kind of therapist. She should know what to do. I find her and tell her I think it would be a good idea for her to speak with Solstice.

"I was speaking with her," Claire says. "She told me about a beautiful vision she had. She said she feels like no one can understand, and I told her, *throughout history, women like you have been misunderstood.*"

There's no way to bridge the chasm between us. I go back to the room. I don't dance or help take down the marquee or clean up the camp. I know that makes me look like a spoiled brat, but whatever. When it's time to go, I survey the empty field. The patch of yellow grass where the marquee was looks like a crop circle.

WE WERE SUPPOSED to leave three hours ago, but as usual, we're delayed. Otto has a bad cough, but he refused to let Kuba take him to the doctor's office. Now he's changed his mind, so we have to wait for him and Kuba to get back from the doctor before we pick up Kuba's mother and Doug and Shanti, who are staying with her, and start our journey.

After a long drive, most of which I sleep through, we arrive at a cute log cabin. About twenty people have come for the ceremony, including Véra and Marie. There are two big rooms where people have set up their sleeping bags and mattresses along the walls. Kuba asks people to move so the English speakers can be together for translation. He puts me next to him, Shanti next to me, and Doug next to Shanti. There's no space for his mother, so she's on the opposite side of the room, and Véra and Marie are in the other room.

The curandero, Dante, is friendly and funny. He calls Kuba Jakubito. There's an apprentice named Sebastian and a few helpers, including a handsome one named Eliáš.

I take a shower, and when I'm getting dressed in one of the bedrooms, Véra comes in and sits on the bed. I ask how she is. "I have a hard time with Tadeáš," she says. "He is mean to me and to my son."

"Is it hard for you to see him with . . ."

"No," she says. "My son is twelve, and when that idiot told him he will be a big brother, he said, *Congratulations to you for ruining your life.*"

So Solstice is pregnant. That makes our encounter in the field so much more disturbing.

"You know," Véra says. "I see you now, and it's like seeing myself ten years ago. It's so easy to lose yourself."

"But Kuba isn't Tadeáš," I say.

"No," she says. "And you're not me."

I FIND KUBA outside on a blanket with his mother cuddling him. Something is wrong.

"What happened?" I ask. I sit next to them, and when I take his hand I feel his mother subtly pulling him closer to her.

"Otto probably has a cancer," he says.

I ask him if he wants to go home, and he says no. I ask if he wants a hug, and he says no. "I'm sorry," he says. "If I go into it I will not stop."

He goes to the van, opens the glove box and takes out the conjoined crystals he gave me in New Zealand.

"You found them," I say. I must have left them behind.

He presses them into my hand. "Hold it during the ceremony," he says. "It will protect you. And I will also."

THERE'S A GROUP meeting where we share our intentions, then Dante explains how the night will go. Dante and Sebastian will each be in one of the rooms, and we will be taken to one or the other of them one at a time for "cleaning."

We sit on our beds and wait. There's only candlelight in the room. "Now anyone can come when he is ready," Kuba says. He goes first. He kneels in front of Dante, and Dante gives him the cup. He holds it in front of his chest, then drinks it all. I go next. The taste isn't that bad. It's like old fermented juice.

I return to my mattress and hold my crystals in my right hand. Once everyone has finished drinking, the candles are blown out, and it's completely dark. I thought it would take a long time, but already a warm blue light is radiating through my body. It moves up through my chest into my throat. My mouth falls open. I can feel my pulse in my lips and tongue. The light keeps moving up to my forehead. Some force is going up with it, like I'm in a flower stem and there's energy surging through me. I anticipate bursting out into the daylight. Then Shanti touches my arm, and the light disappears.

I concentrate again. I'm in a rainforest. I see myself from behind. I'm a blue being sitting cross-legged and clutching a diamond in my right hand. Sebastian is in front of me. Not in the vision, in the room. I can feel that it's him even though I can't see him. He's shaking leaves over my head and whistling, and I know he can see what I'm seeing. *Look up.* I tilt my head back and see a sky full of stars. My mouth is hanging open. I've never seen anything so beautiful. What's so special about this? *Nothing. It happens all the time.* Why haven't I seen it before? *You never look.*

Shanti vomits, and I lose my concentration. The vision disappears. I try to focus. I'm at a mall, and I'm being led up the stairs to a rooftop parking lot. Shanti is sniffing. I step out into the light. *Look up.* I let my head fall back, and it's like I'm seeing the sky for the first time. I'm helpless with wonder.

I remember the blue being and the rainforest. I try to concentrate and imagine myself there, and I hear the music that belongs to that place, but then Shanti vomits again, and I lose it. Someone is whispering. I have to pee. I call Eliáš. I feel sick. I vomit, and the taste of it makes me keep vomiting. Someone is standing in front of me. It feels like he's spitting on me. Surely not. I reach out and touch a face. Eliáš. I vomit again. I look up. He's standing now, waving his bright red penis in my face. He helps me to my feet and holds his penis in front of himself as he guides me to the bathroom. I'm amazed by how strong he is and how long and flexible his penis is.

When we get to the bathroom, there's a red nightlight, and I can see that his penis is not a penis but a torch. He says, "I will be waiting when you come out." I'm so touched by this. My lips are chattering. I go in. I hear swishing and shushing sounds all around me. I wonder if Eliáš can hear me in here. I sit on the toilet and pee, then I have to vomit again, so I get off the toilet and vomit into it.

Eliáš leads me to a mattress that isn't mine. "This isn't my place," I whisper.

"Yes it is," he says. I sit on the mattress and reach for my sleeping bag, but it's gone, and Eliáš is gone too. Shanti is next to me. I can tell it's her because of her sniffing. She must have been taken to the wrong place, too. She touches me, and it's like being electrocuted. I reach for my sleeping bag. I can't find it. I know this story. There's no way to get the sleeping bag. I have to freeze.

I try to remember what I was doing before I went to the toilet. I can see Eliáš' penis again. It looks like he's peeing into someone's bucket. I laugh, and I hear Kuba laughing, too. He must be seeing the same thing. Other people laugh. They must see it, too. Or are they laughing about their own things? Of course they are. And he isn't peeing, he's pouring water. That isn't his penis, it's his torch. I know this story.

There's music again. I'm so cold. I reach for my sleeping bag, and this time I get it. I find the top, put my feet inside and pull, but it only comes up to my ankles. I pull again, and it's up to my knees. I pull again, but it won't come further. It doesn't work. I'm so tired! I pull again. Nothing. I can't keep going.

I wave my hand from side to side, and each time I'm touching different things in nature, leaves and rocks and bark and water, and the music in the room corresponds with everything I touch.

I see myself on a bus. I'm smiling. *Sometimes you smile even when you're not happy.*

So what? Don't smile?

No! Be happy!

Doug moans, "I want to stop the process."

"What?" says Shanti.

"I want to stop the process."

Shanti vomits then touches my arm again. I jerk my body away to show her how much she's upsetting me. I try again with the sleeping bag, but it's hopeless.

"Can you pass me a tissue?" Shanti says.

"Ah! Wuh?" Doug says. "What was that?"

"A *tissue.*"

"What?"

I feel compassion for them, but it's like they're on an island where no one can reach them, and they are so annoying.

"I have to bail," Doug says.

"You need a pail?"

"Ah! Shanti! I want to stop the process. How to do it?"

"What?"

"How to do it?"

"Do what?" She vomits again. "Oh, I need a tissue."

"Ugh, I need a bucket," Doug says.

"Here," someone whispers.

"This is *not* my bucket," Doug says. "It stinks terribly."

I close my eyes and try to communicate telepathically with Eliáš. *Help them.*

Soon, comes the answer. Can he hear my thoughts?

I'm attracted to you, I tell him in my head.

I'm not here to flirt with other people's girlfriends. He's right. Shame on me. I try to concentrate on the rainforest again, but I can't because Doug and Shanti won't shut up, and Shanti won't stop touching me and sniffing.

I move to the back of my mattress, as far away from Shanti as possible, and sit up straight. I see a man looking out through a slit in a wall. Outside the wall are warriors with spears.

Don't be afraid.

What's going to happen?

If I want to know, I have to go through it myself. I have to *be* him. I agree, and now I'm in the man's body looking out through the wall. *No!*

I see a blonde woman tucking her hair behind her ear, a toilet paper roll rolling down a hallway, an alligator with its snout stuck in a trap. There are stories that lead to these images, but I forget the stories until the images recur, and I discover that I'm cycling through the same meaningless nonsense over and over again. The blonde woman tucks her hair behind her ear. I say, "That's enough," but it's relentless. The alligator, the toilet paper, the woman . . .

I seem to be moving on. I'm being led up, being told to look up, and I see the sky like it's the first time, and I feel so amazed, and so relieved to have moved on, but then Shanti touches me.

Damn it!

She whispers, "Mája, can you move a bit?"

"Why?"

"You're on my bed." That's wrong, but I move just to get away from her. "Keep going," she says. I move again. "More," she says.

"I can't!"

"More," she says. I move one more time. "More," she says. "A bit more," she whispers.

"It's too hard," I say, and I wrap myself in whatever is close to me that feels like a sleeping bag.

Eliáš says, "I'm going to move you the other way." He holds my wrists and drags me to the other side of the room. I have a few seconds of peace, then Shanti whispers, "Can you move?"

What is she even doing here on the other side of the room? I try to move a bit, but I'm not sure if I have actually moved. Shanti is quiet. Finally she's satisfied. But now someone is holding my wrists again. It must be Eliáš taking me back to Shanti, and she's going to be angry, but it's not my fault!

"This is totally fucked up!" I say to the floor.

"Shhhh," someone says.

I feel singled out for punishment. There must be a place for me somewhere! Why won't they leave me alone?

As soon as Eliáš is gone, the repeating images come back. The toilet paper, the woman tucking her hair behind her ear. There are sounds that go with them. Exactly at the awful moment when I realise I've seen this all hundreds of times before, I hear scratching, retching, clicking, Kuba screaming. His screams seem to fill the whole house, but it's in my head, because he's next to me.

"That's enough," I say firmly. I tap on my forehead. "Enough." There's something there blocking me. I rub my forehead, trying to get it off. I have to vomit again, so I lean over the bucket, but nothing comes out. I keep my head the bucket, waiting to vomit and rubbing my forehead against the rim. I see myself on the bus again. I'm smiling. *You'll be happier if you're more natural. You don't have to pretend.*

Eliáš is whispering. "I can move her if you want," he says. I freeze. Is he saying he'll take me away? Without taking my head out of the bucket, I reach for my sleeping bag, but it isn't there.

I reach the other way and touch part of someone's body. I pull my hand back. I don't want Eliáš to take me away.

I close my eyes. Lights and shapes, but no more visions. I'm almost asleep, my head is still in the bucket. *How can you expect to manage your thoughts in this situation if you can't sit in meditation for ten minutes?* It's true. My thoughts are repetitive garbage. "That's so true," I say. I'm nodding *yes, yes, yes.* I understand. I get it. I know what to do. I'm still nodding with my head in my bucket when Eliáš kneels next to me and says, "Mája, it's time for cleaning."

"I'm vomiting."

"You can vomit there." I'm lifted up. Is he carrying me? It's so nice to let myself sink into him. I remember Kuba, and he's beside me. We're kneeling in front of Dante like a bride and groom. I still have my crystals in my hand. I have to vomit again. I lean forward, and a bucket appears. While I'm vomiting, Dante shakes leaves over me and does something with my forehead and the back of my head. He seems to be sucking something from my crown and spitting it out. Whatever he's doing, I appreciate it so much. I squeeze the crystals, and I feel such fondness for Kuba, just as a person, not what he is to me. I want to tell him I'm sorry for being impatient and demanding. I've been depending on him too much.

WE OPEN OUR eyes at the same time. I'm in his sleeping bag. I wish I could stay here with him all day, but he says he has to take a shower, and we're not supposed to have any physical contact.

The room looks like the aftermath of a violent orgy. I get into my own sleeping bag, close my eyes and picture myself as the blue being in the rainforest. I try to focus on my breathing. I wonder if Kuba will meet Marie in the shower? I try counting my breaths. I make it to three.

"The hell room," Doug says. He's standing in the doorway. "The dungeon."

"How was your night?" I ask. He sits on his mattress.

"Shanti was just sick. She was lucky. I spent the whole night seeing these . . . pictures."

"Of what?"

"Ugh, cops and robbers, tractors, other vehicles . . . honestly I'm trying not to think about it. You had an active night."

"What do you mean?"

"You were all over the place, lying on everyone, trying to steal their sleeping bags, and their beds."

"Shanti was in *my* bed."

He shakes his head. "You were in hers. You were in everybody's."

"Was I?" We both laugh. It feels good to laugh at myself.

I have to crawl to the toilet. I hold onto the sink and look at myself in the mirror. My hair is greasy. My concealer came off during the night. It's funny it's called concealer. I've never thought about that before.

One of the scars on my cheek has turned purple. I still look gaunt and ill, but my eyes are so clear. I raise my hand to my face and stroke my cheek. I say, "I love you, Mája."

The others are talking at the table outside. Someone is playing a guitar. Through the window I see the sky. I remember the bus smiling thing from my visions. *Be happy.* I'm tired of hiding in bathrooms, grasping mirrors behind doorways. I will go out there as myself and be happy.

No one reacts to the sight of me. Of course they don't. No one cares. I make a cup of tea and sit at the far end of the table so my good side is to the group.

It's only that now I appreciate how intimate last night was, and I feel timid, like I'm seeing a new lover in the daylight. Eliáš sits across from me. I remember our telepathic communication. I hope that wasn't real.

After breakfast, we meet in a circle to discuss what we experienced. When it's my turn, Sebastian says, "You were having visions very quickly."

"Yes," I say. "I felt like you could see what I was seeing."

He nods. "You were surrounded by beautiful stars."

I FIND KUBA making a black cord necklace for my crystals.

"How was your night, my love?" he asks.

"Amazing, I think. How was yours?"

"I was on the toilet almost whole night, screaming."

So that was him. "What happened?"

"I was vomiting from myself. It's so hard to see all my shits. I always think I'm on the end of it, but then ayahuasca shows me more, and every time I'm surprised by my fakeness."

I actually feel the opposite. I'm surprised by my realness.

"I have something for you," he says. He takes out his phone and reads me a text from his friend saying that a French doctor who lives in Peru is coming to Prague to speak at a conference. I ask what his name is, but I already know.

"That's him," I say. "The one I told you about. From the video."

Kuba nods. "You would like to go there?" he says.

"Yes. But do you remember? He's the doctor who lives in Peru, and I watched that video where he talks about the myths, and I couldn't find the ending?"

"Oh yes," Kuba says. "Great."

I ask how Otto is.

"He won't go to a hospital, so we will see," Kuba says.

He puts the cord over my head and tightens it so the crystals rest in the notch at the base of my throat, just above the pendant he gave me for my birthday.

It's the first time I've let him see me without makeup in the daylight. "Beauty," he says. It's hard to believe it, but I try.

"When I saw you with Eliáš, I started to question myself,"

he says. "I was thinking I'm not good enough, because I saw someone else is interesting person for you. That was part of the reason why I have to be alone this morning, because I have to stay connected with myself so I won't follow those fears."

"It's funny, because meanwhile I was in the bathroom looking in the mirror and wondering if I'm good enough."

"So you are also having this conversation with mirrors," he says. "I think everyone is."

"Why Eliáš?" I ask.

He smiles. "What your heart feels, my heart knows."

Autumn

I ASSUMED KUBA'S schedule would slow down as the weather got colder, but instead his work seems to double, and he's getting invitations to facilitate workshops and retreats abroad, too.

I'm taking a Czech language course, and I'm learning to get around Prague on my own. Sometimes I have coffee with Véra after class. We don't have much in common, but I like her company. I've been weaning myself off makeup. Kuba doesn't seem to notice. "Someone overcuted you" is his new favourite expression. When he's home, he's too tired to do much, so our days are usually peaceful. But if he's home for more than two days, we enter into a cycle—talk about the future, what our relationship means, his dreams about the farmhouse in South Bohemia, my fear I wouldn't be happy with that life.

When the credits rolled on *Želary*, he was crying. He said, "Májenka, I want to ask you to please consider to stay here with me. I am part of this land, I belong here." I would have thought that being here would help me relate to this kind of sentiment, but if anything it's only becoming more foreign to me.

His mother tried to find my family's graves. She called all the administrators in charge of the cemeteries in České Budějovice. It's a huge city, my family's names are very common, and people have to pay rent for graves in the Czech Republic, so there's a strong possibility that the grave was replaced if no one was paying for it, assuming it existed in the first place. Even if it does exist, it's just a piece of stone. The fact that she tried so hard to find it means more to me than the grave itself would have.

KUBA CONVINCES ME to take a few short trips before it gets too cold. We visit his grandmother's cottage. I make a drum at one of his workshops. We take a bike trip, which is romantic but also a bit stressful, because we sleep in fields and often get woken in the morning by farm machinery.

During the day, we picnic by shrines and rivers and hide from the rain in hunting lookouts. Kuba pushes me up steep hills, makes campfires, and sings me songs. He's teaching me the words to Kometa. He sent his parents a recording of me saying the most difficult part, which he says I pronounce perfectly.

In Třeboň, he takes me to a fancy restaurant, gives me an envelope and says, "Happy name day, lásko."

I haven't celebrated my name day since I was a child. In the envelope are tickets to a Nohavica concert that starts in an hour. It's weird that I never thought about it before, but I'm surprised Nohavica is alive. Like Leonard, he seems too legendary to be among us.

We ride our bikes to the venue, a park next to a château. In person, Nohavica looks like a dishevelled Václav Havel. His voice has the same deeply reassuring, paternal quality as Leonard's, and like Leonard's, his lyrics transmit truths we probably all know but could never put so well. Then he sings this shocking thing, which I have to get Kuba to repeat because I don't believe it the first time, and I'm reminded that it's foolish to idolise anyone.

Kuba takes out his phone. It's a message from Pavla with lyrics to a song Nohavica wrote about his son, Jakub. Since camp, she's been writing to Kuba daily. I told him what she said when she came to our room, and he seemed angry. He wrote her that he wants to have a break from communicating with her, but he hopes the angels are taking care of her. She responded that she was deleting him from her phone and she sends shit on his angels. She also said she will never speak to me again, which is fine with me.

Despite her proclamations, she writes to Kuba all the time, and her tone varies wildly from one message to the next. Most disturbingly, the content of her messages often suggests she knows what we're doing. The day we left for our bike trip, she sent him a photo of her and Adam on a bike trip. When we accidentally borrowed two left hiking boots from a family friend, she wrote him, *I heard Mája has two left feet.* Now this.

WE BRING KUBA'S mother chocolates to thank her for looking for my family's graves. She's made us a small feast, none of which I can eat. His father reads in the corner instead of joining us at the table.

His mother pushes my plate toward me. "Eat," she says.

"Thank you so much," I say. I ask Kuba to explain to her that there are some things I can't eat and maybe find a nice way to tell her that I don't want to talk about it.

He tells her, and she smiles and jiggles my wrist. "To je blbost, Májo," she says. I ask Kuba what it means, and he says it's not important.

Kuba's father comes over and places the book he was reading on the table in front of me. He's made a newspaper sleeve for it, so it's not until I open the cover that I realise it's my first novel.

"Fine," he says. He shakes my hand, kisses his wife, hugs Kuba, and goes to bed. I flip through the book. He's underlined words in pencil and written notes in Czech in the margins. I didn't even realise he spoke English. Then again, I don't get the impression that speaking is his forté in any language.

I hear Kuba and his mother say Pavla's name several times. I ask what they're talking about. Kuba says Pavla invited him to go to a tea room with her, and he didn't respond, so she called his mother and asked her to persuade him.

"Is that what she's doing? Trying to persuade you?"

"Yes, but I won't go."

"Why is she interfering?" I ask. "Are they friends?"

His mother, who understands none of this, is beaming at me.

"They were always big enemies, but since I stopped to co-operate with Pavla, they start to be friends."

Kuba says something to his mother, and her face falls. "I told her not to talk about Pavla more."

"It's not talking *about* her that's the problem. It's talking *to* her about you when you don't want to communicate with her. Does she know that you asked Pavla for a break?" He says something to his mother, and she looks at me when she answers.

"She said she does not talk to Pavla about us," he says.

"She doesn't, or she won't?"

"Both."

In the van, Kuba checks his phone. Pavla has written to him twelve times in the past hour. The first message says she's calling him, then she's coming over, she's at the gate. The series ends with a handwritten note stuck to our door with chewing gum. It says, *Oh no, the witch is here!*

"Oh my God, she's a stalker," I say. He doesn't know what it means, so I look it up on Google Translate.

"It's not so bad," he says.

My phone dings. An email from Pavla. It says, "Please, Mája. Peace." I ask Kuba how she got my email address.

"From some group emails, probably," he says.

"Your mother must have told her what I said."

"My love," he says.

"Otherwise why would she write me that now?"

I ask him to call his mother, and she admits she gave Pavla my email address so she could write to me and sort things out and we can all spend Christmas together.

"That's so disrespectful!" I say. Kuba looks at me like *calm down*. "That doesn't seem wrong to you?"

"She just want to be kind," he says.

"It's not unkind to have boundaries!"

He says, "I will do everything to make this safe space for you, my love."

I GOT THE grant I applied for before I left Canada. I can't keep living off my Visa, so it comes as a relief, but on the other hand it means I'm supposed to write an uplifting story about a Canadian woman travelling to the Czech Republic in search of her roots, and I'm not sure I'm any more capable of that than I am of finishing my other novel. Probably the clever thing would be to write something with mass appeal and use the money to build a turtle bunker or fortified forest garden. Of course that's the kind of selfish individualism that got us into the mess we're in, but I would do it if I knew how to write something with mass appeal, which I don't.

It seems like other writers have this broad perspective that lets them locate what they're doing within a specific tradition and within the whole history of literature, but no matter how much I read, I remain almost completely in the dark on both. I mean, how could you possibly read enough Canadian short stories to answer the question, "What do you think about the state of the short story in Canada?" Or how could anyone say of a book that, "Nothing like this has ever been written"? Have you read everything that's ever been written? Some people certainly talk as if they have.

Kuba seems hurt when I tell him I want to rearrange the space so I can work. He describes how he spent days cleaning our room before I arrived, and when he'd finished, he went downstairs so he could come back up and imagine what it would be like for me to see it for the first time. "I came in the door and said . . . this is terrible!"

"It's not terrible," I say. "I just need my own space."

He helps me to make part of the loft into an office, and he builds me a meditation area, which I decorate with cushions and pillows and a stool that serves as a table. He gives me a life-sized plaster cherub head to use as a bookend for my mini-library. He also convinced Otto to set live traps for the mice and relocate them to the forest. And he's looking into getting a door for the bathroom.

Every morning I wake up, make myself tea, try to meditate for half an hour, then sit down to write, but I always fall asleep during my meditation, and I never get more than ten minutes of not-writing done before I'm engrossed in news coverage of the refugee crisis.

I can't help feeling skeptical about the public displays of generosity toward the refugees, which seem self-serving in that painting-an-orphanage way that overlooks the complicity of the giver, the full humanity of the recipient, and the unsolvable complexity of the whole situation. Then again, passing out teddy bears and bottled water—the perfect symbol of our wasteful, petroleum dependent lifestyles—is better than what I'm doing, which is sitting behind my laptop in a warm room with passports to three of the safest countries on earth, critiquing the ways other people are trying to help. So since I can't do nothing, and I don't know what's the right thing to do, I use my Visa to donate to the Red Cross and MSF, feel some relief, and keep watching.

KUBA AND I take the train and then a tram to the venue where Mabit is speaking. He delivers his presentation in Spanish, Kuba translates the Czech translator into English for me, and I think we both miss a lot.

At the break, Kuba goes to make a phone call, and I work up the courage to introduce myself to Mabit. I ask him in French if he would be willing to tell me more about his theory about the myths, and he agrees. We sit outside in the garden, where refreshments are being served.

He says that in his view, different mythical horizons predominate in different epochs. "That is myth in the positive sense of the word," he says. "As the most elevated spiritual and cultural horizon of a society."

Tribal societies, he says, are governed by the myth of Justice, and westernised societies by the myth of Love. In the tribal context, the centre of identification is the group, and group members seek an equilibrium of reciprocity with the external world, other tribes, the divine, spirits, plants, and animals. The westernised worldview, on the other hand, centres the individual, turning the focus inward, "So the question becomes, *How do I solve myself?*"

He says that myths arise, become established, and decline in stages, and in the process they reveal their shadows and limitations. Now we are experiencing both the waning of the myth of Love and the infancy of the myth of Freedom, and at this threshold, he says, there is a great deal of confusion and contradiction. He says you see this in the New Age mentality, for example, which he calls an imitation of the myth of Freedom situated in the myth of Love.

I ask if he can talk more about the myth of Freedom. He says that when it becomes established it will marry the highest ideals of the myths of Justice and Love—interdependence and individuation—but at this stage, true freedom is not yet well-understood.

"True freedom is a paradox," he says. "Because it's about surrender. What are your resources? Your qualities? Your inheritances? Your gifts? What are the things that only you can use to say thank you to life? That's vocation. When you find that, you are obliged to forgo all the rest. So you are imprisoned by your calling, but in it you find freedom."

I ask him how he thinks the myth of Freedom will become established.

"I have the impression that it will manifest not by something grandiose and universal," he says, "but by people liberating themselves, each following their own path. If there's a critical mass, a small number will suffice. Even one person can occasion a considerable change, because they can go straight to the goal, and that can enter deeply into the spirit of the world."

Kuba joins us, and I introduce them. Mabit asks Kuba what he does for a living, and Kuba talks about dances and how all religions teach the same truths. I've never seen anyone look at Kuba the way Mabit does. It isn't unkind, there's something tender about it, but it's *knowing*.

IN THE TRAM, Kuba turns on his phone. More texts from Pavla. He starts reading them to me, but I'm not listening. I'm thinking about what Mabit said about vocation. *What are the things that only you can use to say thank you to life?* I bet I would be able to answer that question if I had a father like him. Then again, whatever his personal faults, my father has made films that have had tangible, positive impacts on other people's lives, which is more than I can say about anything I've done. And I'm an adult now, I need to find my own answers. I've been wallowing in self-doubt forever. I need to get over myself. Contribute somehow. Stop moving around, consuming, having experiences, waiting for real life to start. I have to write something useful, go back to comms work, or train as something else. A social worker? No, I would be terrible at that. Comms work, then. And as for Kuba, if we can't resolve our geographical dilemma, I will leave him. It's as simple as that.

I was probably supposed to draw a more profound conclusion from my conversation with Mabit. I'm sure it will come to me years from now, when I don't need it any more. I guess it's nice to know that someone believes in the future. I'm so weary of hopelessness, even if it's warranted.

Nohavica has a song where the speaker says if he'd been born a hundred years earlier he would have been looking forward to a long, beautiful twentieth century—it's good that we can't see what the future holds. Yet here we are, in a world that has ended again and again, and some people still believe that we're *on the good way*, as Kuba would say.

Winter

KUBA HAS GONE to Denmark for a dance retreat. Without him this place is so depressing. I walk to Penny Market, sit by the lake, cook boring meals for myself and Otto, worry, read. Not books. I don't have the attention span any more. I read articles. Sometimes I spend the whole day reading different takes on various uncomfortable topics, tying myself in knots with guilt and confusion and exasperation, and finding nowhere to stand, because I agree and disagree with almost everyone. I can't talk to anyone about this, even Becca, so instead I scour comments sections, changing my mind over and over again, and ending up feeling more guilty, confused, and exasperated than ever.

Facebook used to be an escape from my overthinking, but now it's full of reminders of Kuba's women. I type in his name. He has five new friends today, all women and one peacock-type. I scroll through her profile pictures, checking the boxes. Feather earrings, meditation selfie, sacred geometry, big cat (panther), majestic bird (eagle), celestial body (the moon), partially-clothed women's group.

I open Word and re-read what I wrote last night in a little fever of resolution:

1. I will not follow him around to his workshops any more.
2. I will not organise my life around him when he's home.
3. I will meditate for at least fifteen minutes a day.
4. I will write for at least two hours a day.
5. After India, a decision has to be made.
6. I have to decide if I'm going to India.

I GO FOR a walk and spend a long time sitting on a bench watching people fishing for carp in a pond. The pond is artificial, the carp, the traditional Czech Christmas food, are originally from Asia, and it's hardly a sport to catch them, because they've been bred and stocked for harvesting. But they don't know that. There's probably a useful metaphor in this. Something about everything being a facsimile, something false standing in for something true, but under the surface of the lie another, dormant truth.

Back at home, I hear the now familiar sound of Otto banging on the metal pipes. I come to the door of his room, and he hugs himself and shivers. His fire must have gone out. I bring wood and start to rebuild the fire. "No, no, no," he says as I'm breaking up the kindling. I open the door of the stove, and he says, "No! Hazard!" He sniffs the air, then he makes an explosion gesture with his hands and says, "Boom! Gone."

"What?"

He lifts a shaking finger, and I follow it. He seems to be pointing at the skylight, but there's nothing there. I look around. There's a mouse in a live trap on the stove. Its tail has been damaged by the closing mechanism. I pick up the trap and put it in the bathroom for Kuba to deal with when he gets home. Once Otto's fire is going, I go and get into bed. Maybe something is going to explode, but there's nothing I can do about it if I can't understand him. When I leave, he says, "Nevim, nevim." *I don't know.*

I HEAR THE gate close, Kuba's steps on the stairs. My response is Pavlovian. I'm so well trained. But he doesn't even climb the ladder to kiss me. He says, "I have to keep going before I collapse."

When he comes back, I tell him about the mouse, and we check on it. He lifts the tea towel I put over the trap. "In past, I would help her by killing her," he says. "But one monk told me you should not interfere with the karma of another being unless you want to link your karma to hers."

So much for activism and philanthropy, monk.

Kuba opens the cage and leaves it in the garden. "Hopefully a cat will come and eat her soon," he says.

He goes to check on Otto, and I make us tea. When he comes back, I'm sure he will be with me, but he says he has to check some emails. After half an hour, I climb down the ladder. He has headphones on, so he doesn't hear me. He's writing to someone named Parvati.

I climb back up to the loft and check his Facebook friends for a Parvati, but I can't find anyone with that name.

He gets up and puts on his coat. "I have to go, lásko," he says. "I will be back soon."

"Where are you going?"

"To deliver something."

I can't believe this. I'm here waiting in this room for him, and he can't even stop to sit with me for five minutes. "I missed you," I say. "I hoped we could spend some time together." Already I'm back in barnacle mode. "Are you listening to me?"

He says, "I hear you, but what you are saying is not important for me." He's never said anything like that to me before, and now I feel desperate to find a way back to him. "Please, lásko," he says. "I will be here soon."

He's gone so long that by the time he comes back I'm not even angry any more. I'm prepared to let him come and hold me, and I promise that I won't say anything or ask any questions, but

I don't hear the van door slam or his footsteps on the stairs. I lie awake for a long time before going to the window. I can see him in the van. His face is lit by his cellphone.

I pull on my boots and coat and go downstairs. His head is on the steering wheel. I open the van door. His mouth is open, and a long line of spit is dribbling onto his pants. I reach out to touch him, but he pushes my hand away.

"What is it?" I ask.

"Please," he says. "I have to be alone."

"I'm scared."

He wipes away his spit. "Don't be afraid, Májenka. Please. I have to sleep in the forest. Promiň. I have to go."

"I've been waiting for you!"

"I'm sorry," he says. He's shaking. "I have to go," he says. He starts the van. I step back, he slams the door and drives away.

He returns in the morning smelling of smoke. He climbs up to the bed. I close my computer and cross my arms.

"That was good," he says. "I had to reconnect with the forest."

"Why were you crying?"

He rubs his forehead. "Can you sit with me, lásko?"

I sit across from him in front of his altar. He's so distant. "When I was on the retreat, I had one very strong experience," he says. "There was one leader there what I felt very strong connection with, and we did the shamanic journey together and saw that she was my mother in the past life, and her husband was useless, and I saw that she was repeating this pattern in many lives, having son with useless husband, and now she has young son and useless husband again. So I received this message to tell her that it's time to break this cycle, and we did a constellation together where I played the role of husband for her so she can experience having a strong man next to her."

"What do you mean, played the role of husband for her?"

164

"We were next to each other, and I was being in the position of strong man, and when it happened I felt a huge stream of souls passing through me to some healing from ancient times."

Now he's crying again. I feel sick, and sick of this. "So, sorry, you were doing what with this woman?"

He starts his heaving crying. "I'm sorry," he says. "I can't hold it."

I watch him cry, and when he's finished, he says, "Mája, I want to ask you something."

"Yes."

"I want to ask if you will make the wedding ceremony with me."

He can't be serious. "What do you mean?"

"It means I would like to express to you and to all the souls around that we are together, and to symbolically cut our connections with the others."

"Why?"

"I want clean space for our family life. From both of our sides."

"Kuba! Don't you get that this is impossible? You won't leave here because you're a Czech tree and you need to heal your nation with dances or whatever, and I won't stay here because I hate it!" There, I said it.

"I believe we can find the way," he says. I know what the way is for him. I'll give up and move to South Bohemia and be a little wife with a kerchief on my head while he's off healing all his past-life mothers.

"Why don't you do us both a favour and marry your Czech Mája?" I say. "It sounds like she would fit perfectly into the woman-shaped hole you've been preparing in your life."

"Me and you makes sense for me," he says. "I was waiting for you my whole life."

SHAKING WALLS. PANIC and inflammation. A microscopic war happening inside my body, immune cells rushing into battle against . . . what?

"Kubíku?" My top lip splits. Otto bangs on the pipes. I lick my lips and taste blood.

"Kuba!" I say.

"I don't want to go," he says.

He's been spending most of his time in bed since he got back from Denmark, so now we're rotting together. He isn't interested in socialising, which is fine with me, but I wish he didn't spend so much time with his headphones on.

Otto bangs again. I can't bear that sound. I feel so anxious. I assume he wants cream. I get some from the fridge and bring it to him. He sniffs it, makes a face and hands it back to me. I'm sure it's fresh. He wants Kuba to give it to him.

I get my coat. Kuba doesn't look up from his screen. The fresh air helps, but I have this awful feeling, like I've forgotten something important and there will be consequences. The people I pass on my way to the shop all keep their eyes on the pavement. The shopkeeper doesn't look up from his newspaper.

When Drew and I came to Prague with his parents, his mother and I shopped for souvenirs and went to bookstores and cafés while he and his dad went to museums and pubs. At the end of each day, we traded stories about how rude the Czechs were. "Of course," his father said. "It's a hangover from communism."

"And it makes sense to be xenophobic when you've been occupied three times in the twentieth century alone," Drew added. It seems so arrogant to me now, thinking you can know anything about a place after shopping there for a few days.

When we were in Varanasi, Drew spent part of every day at Manikarnika, the burning ghat. I didn't want to go there. Instead, I sat by the river and watched people swimming, playing cricket, flying kites.

Drew has a freakishly good sense of direction, so I didn't go into the city's labyrinthine streets without him, but one day he took longer than usual at the burning ghat, and I went to browse the shops on my own. I got lost and had to follow a funeral procession to find my way back to the river, which was how I arrived at Manikarnika.

I would have continued back to the guesthouse if a woman hadn't intercepted me to try and extract a donation and Drew hadn't noticed and come to lead me up to a balcony where he'd been watching the fires from above. I scanned the scene. I could see the feet of one burning body. A cow eating marigolds. Wood being delivered on boats.

"Hash? Marijuana? Hash?" Someone hissed sour alcohol breath in my ear. "Twenty-four-hour power, no toilet no shower." I moved away from the drug dealer and stepped into a warm pile of shit. I scraped my sandal on the stones, told Drew I had to pee, and walked back to the guesthouse alone. On the way, I saw an injured monkey sitting in a corner. A holy man's followers were watching television nearby. I asked one of them what had happened to the monkey, and he said it was electrocuted running on the wires above and fell and broke its legs.

I went closer. When it saw me, it cowered and cradled its legs. They moved, and it attacked them, not understanding that they were part of its body. When it felt the bite of its own teeth, it stopped attacking itself and cradled its legs again. Back at the guesthouse, I sat on the toilet crying hysterically. Drew thought someone had died until I managed to explain about the monkey. I kept thinking about how it held its legs after it attacked them. It was so human and so hopeless.

Otto smells the new bottle of cream and puts it on the table without tasting it. I tell Kuba he has to check on Otto, and I get back into bed. I open my computer and try to write an email to Becca, but I end up staring at my reflection in Photobooth.

I'm so ugly. I don't know how Kuba can like me.

He's playing the piano for Otto. His voice is different than usual. I close my eyes and listen. This song corresponds with something in me, like a key in a lock that opens centuries of sadness. When he's finished, he comes to the door and looks up at me. Both of our faces are wet with tears. He climbs the ladder. "What was it about?" I ask.

"There were soldiers marching through one particular valley," he says. "And they meet a girl carrying veggies, and they say, *Hey you girl, you will remember this place for the rest of your life.* And one week later she was crying a lot, and one month later she was crying even more, and one year later she was walking on the meadow carrying her son in her hands, and she said, *Oh my dear son, what should I do with you? Should I raise you up, or should I drown you in the river?* And he answers, *Hey my mother, raise me up, and put me to the army to be a soldier,* and then it continues again in this valley there were the soldiers marching, and they noticed the girl who carried the veggies."

"I feel like you can tell what it's about without understanding the words."

"That's the transmission," he says. "I believe if the artists connect to some source they can hook on and receive things, and the messages what they transmit are not only in the words, but in the music also."

His phone beeps. He looks at it and puts it away.

"Pavla?"

"Yes."

"What does it say?"

He takes it out again. "There are two," he says. "In the first she say she is one millimetre from the enlightenment, and she doesn't want to say too much about it, she just wants me to know. Then later she asks me to remove all my Facebook pictures where she is."

"I'm not going to India," I say.

"Why?"

"Because there's no point. And I don't want to be a tourist any more."

I'VE BEEN SLEEPING too much. Kuba is busy all the time again. I feel no motivation to do anything, and I can't stand thinking any more, so I sleep.

Otto's friend Sophie has hitchhiked here to spend Christmas with him. She gives Kuba and me an ornament she made, an angel with flaming red wings. She says there are flowers inside. "Lilies, for heartbreak."

"You mean they will break our hearts or fix them?" I ask.

She says, "Let's hope for both."

I give her some candy from the care package Gina sent me, and I enjoy watching her sample chocolate fish and pineapple lumps as if they were exotic delicacies.

We fill the van with food and gifts and begin our journey to "the little village of two churches," as Kuba calls it, where Kuba and Ondra's families have spent Christmas since Kuba was a child.

On the way, Kuba wants to go to a winter solstice celebration. I'm already meeting so many new people at Christmas, I don't want to meet more people on the way there. It's also the middle of winter, and he's planning for us to sleep in the van.

"Isn't it too cold?" I ask.

"Freezing is actually better," he says. "If there was snow but it was warm, it would mean everything would get wet. And we have three sleeping bags and four blankets, and there is insulation in the walls of the van, and I can boil unlimited amount of water on the gas stove, so I can make sure you will be warm. We just need to dress warm for the actual ceremony."

He's wearing thick, cream-coloured woolen clothing with embroidery at the neck and cuffs and a black scarf and hat. I'm wearing three layers of sweatpants and a fawn puffer jacket.

We get lost and arrive late. We park in a field with other cars and vans and climb a hill toward the sound of fiddle and bagpipes—or dudy, as Kuba corrects me when I ask why people are playing bagpipes at a Slavic ceremony. At the top of the hill people are dancing around a central fire with four smaller fires around it. Kuba introduces me to a friend of his who speaks English, and I stay and chat with her while he goes to drum. I ask her what's happening here.

"The main ceremony is over," she says. "Later there will be a naming ceremony."

"Are the ceremonies from pagan times?" I ask.

"Different people would give different answers," she says. "I would say that Slavic paganism was so overlaid by bloody Christianity it's probably not possible to untangle it, but if it meets people's needs now, maybe it's not so important where it comes from."

She goes to dance, and I watch the flames. I don't know where Kuba went. When he finally appears again, I tell him I'm ready for bed. He says he has to wait for the leader to finish something, because he wants to give him a gift. I wait longer, get colder. When the guy comes back to the fire, Kuba takes me to meet him. They speak in Czech, he gives the guy the gift, which looks like a stone, they hug, and the guy gives him a drum to play. Kuba looks at me apologetically, sits next to the guy, and starts playing.

When we're in the van, I tell him that I didn't like how he started playing the drum after he told me we could leave.

"I know, my love," he says. "But this is something unique, and it was big effort to get here."

"I didn't ask to come here," I say.

He looks wounded.

"I'm sorry," I say. "I don't even understand what this is, or if you're part of it. Are you part of it?"

"I appreciate what they do," he says. "But it is not my way, because I want to work for the unity, and I don't want to call on those old gods, because I don't have any relationship with them."

"Who do you have a relationship with?"

"You. I call on you a lot."

"You know what I mean."

"I have a relationship with the spirit of the forest by our house, for example. But I don't have a name for that, and I don't have an authority who would teach me about it."

"I'm just over meeting new people," I say.

"I wanted to make the best programme for you, my love," he says. "But now I see I was doing it also for myself, because I want you to see how much friends I have and how much interesting things I know about."

"I would be happy to just have dinner or a campfire now and then with your real friends," I say. "Like Ondra. But there's no time because you're always busy with hundreds of clients and acquaintances or so exhausted that you have to stay in bed for days."

"It's nice idea," he says. "And now we're going to spend one week with real friends in mountains, and you will see how cosy life can be."

WE'RE STAYING IN a cottage with honest-to-goodness hay in the mattresses. Ondra's family is here, including his parents, his many brothers and their wives and children. When three more families arrive, there are so many people I give up trying to remember their names, but they all seem lovely.

We hike into the forest and choose a tree to decorate with candles and ornaments. If I give it my full attention, I can usually figure out the general topic of conversation, and I find myself involuntarily matching my facial expression to the tone of what's being said, smiling when something seems to be funny, even though I don't understand.

After the hike, I Skype with Gina in the van. Kuba has set me up with a hot water bottle, sleeping bag, and heater. Gina asks if we're going to India and says she might meet us there. I tell her I'm not going. I don't know about Kuba.

I tell her how difficult I find his lifestyle, how anxious I've been feeling, how I don't know what to do next. She says, "I hope you've told him this."

"A bit."

"That's why you have that problem with your tongue," she says. "You're not speaking your truth."

I'm not sure I have a truth, or if it even matters. I'm interested in *the* truth, if there is such a thing, but my hunch is that when you know it, there isn't much to say.

"Why do you think my mother stayed in Vancouver?" I ask. "If she loved it here so much, why not come back?"

"I can't answer that," Gina says.

"You can't, or you won't?"

"She was living with a very deceitful, dishonest person, and she wasn't well. I don't think she was capable of much, is what I mean."

"Well, it's nice to think she died believing in paradise on earth. If she came back here she might have seen things differently."

"Or maybe one day you will," Gina says.

Kuba knocks on the van door. "My love," he says. "It's time."

I tell Gina I have to go. "Here's an exercise," she says. "Pick up the first book you see, flip through it until you feel drawn to a page, then open it and read the first paragraph your eyes land on. That will be your answer."

WE LEAVE AT twilight. The air smells of coal fires, and we can hear the organ in the distance. We follow narrow paths through the snow to a church on a hill next to a graveyard lit by lanterns. Inside the church smells of frankincense, and there are wooden sleighs dripping onto the carpet at the entrance. The downstairs is packed, so we climb a spiral staircase to the balcony and find places in a creaking wooden pew.

Kuba gives me a songbook and explains the play acted by children wearing homemade angel wings. I'm surprised to find that I recognise the rhythms of the service, even in another language. It's still so much a part of me, even though I'm not part of it any more.

After the service, Kuba takes me to the edge of the cemetery as the bells are starting to ring, and in the darkness we can see the silhouettes of deer escaping into the forest as the echo of the bells swells through the valley.

When the parishioners have gone, the organist gives us the key to the church, and Kuba plays the organ so loudly the building seems to shake. His mother puts her arm around my waist and sways me to the music. Kuba asks what my favourite carol is. I tell him O Holy Night, and I have to hum a bit for him to know what I mean. Apparently there are no Czech words, so I sing the English words quietly to myself. I'm amazed that I remember them all, and I well up at, "Let all within us praise His holy name."

My mother's disappearance ended my relationship with the Church. I never wore the white silk dress or felt the paper-thin wafer on my tongue. I figured if God was planning to punish me, he'd already done it, and in any case, I was starting to have more imminent fears. Some nights I woke up from my nightmares paralysed, knowing that there was someone in my room but unable to scream for help. One night there was snow falling outside my window, and I was convinced that the outside world was under an enchantment, and if I got dragged out there I would never be able to come back.

I didn't tell anyone about those episodes. I must have known that Gina would make too much of them, my father too little. But even though they were terrorising, they stirred up something in me that Teta Běta's God never could, something innate and familiar but also completely mysterious, like the *all within us* in O Holy Night.

BACK AT THE cottage, the fire is still going. Four tables have been pushed together, and by each place there's a gingerbread rocking horse with a name piped onto it in white icing. The room smells of fish, and in the middle of the table are a variety of potato salads. Potato salad with onion, without onion, with salami, with pickles, without mayonnaise, with apples. In the corner of the room is a branch of a fir tree with piles of gifts underneath. At the table, Kuba lifts my plate to show me that there are carp scales under it, for wealth, I think. Or good luck.

After dinner, we watch a creepy fairy tale followed by the president's Christmas message, in which he calls the refugee crisis an organised invasion. Kuba's mother says something, and I ask Kuba to translate.

"She says all the world is responsible for all the world, and we have to watch our thoughts and our opinions and take care of each other," he says. I agree with her. But how?

We switch off the television and put on our warm clothes, then we climb the hill to the tree we decorated. Ondra carries his double bass and Kuba his guitar. After we light the candles, we gather around the tree to sing songs.

Ondra walks with me on the way back. He has his double bass strapped to him, and he holds my arm on the slippery hill. When we get to the cottage, we unwrap gifts, which takes hours, and I sink into the impression that this is a pleasant dream taking place in an enchanted, snowy world.

Late at night, when the dishes are put away and the others are in bed, I find Kuba and Ondra in the cellar. They have old handmade comic books spread out in front of them, and they're laughing, but their eyes are wet. Kuba says, "We are crying for how beautiful childhood we had, and that our friend died, and our parents will die, and nothing will ever come back."

"**OTTO FORGOT HIS** memory," Kuba says. I look at the clock. I must have been having a nightmare. Anxiety through the roof. "Can you come and see him?"

I climb down the ladder and put on Kuba's boots. Otto is sitting up in his bed. He looks awful. "This is Mája," Kuba says. "Do you remember her?"

Otto points at the woodstove.

Yep, he knows who I am.

I go back to bed, but before I fall asleep Otto bangs on the pipes again. Kuba goes next door, and a few seconds later he comes back to call an ambulance. "He is shaking like I have never seen a person shake," he says.

The paramedics arrive, and I hear Otto shouting. Kuba is on the landing. "What's going on?" I ask.

"Otto says he doesn't have a cancer and everything is fine," Kuba says. "They are advising him to come to the hospital, and they are telling him there are other options beside a chemoterapie, but he says no. They can't force him. He says he wants to die. Then they say, *say it again and we can call different kind of doctors and take you to the other hospital.* So he's saying he is joking."

When the paramedics leave, Kuba accuses Otto of pretending to have lost his memory.

"He wants you to be close to him," I say.

He says, "I am fucking tired, and he doesn't listen." Then he goes back to Otto's room, and soon I hear them laughing.

SOPHIE IS HERE. Otto is going to stay at her cottage in the mountains for a week, and after that he has agreed to go to the hospital. Kuba will drive them to her house and stay with them for two nights. He's been playing piano for Otto all morning. We packed his things and cleaned his room, and the disturbed dust particles hover halo-like in the sunlight around Kuba's head as he plays.

Kuba helps Otto down to the car. When they're gone, I go into Otto's room and touch the figures scratched into the wood above the fireplace, following the lines through their impaled bodies with my finger. I should have asked him why this image was so important to him. What he thinks it means.

"I have an intuitive message for you," Sophie says. I startle, because I didn't know she was still here. "I don't know if I should deliver it."

"Well you have to now."

"It's not easy to be psychic," she says. "But when you have a message you know is for someone, you have to tell them."

"Go on then."

"I want to tell you it's not wrong to be angry."

"What do I have to be angry about?"

"I'm not sure," she says. "But my intuition about you is you're afraid that if you get angry you'll never stop."

Spring

I WANT TO run out there and scream *Bullshit! Lies!* Instead I'm peeling potatoes. We're at a week-long dance retreat. I agreed to come at the last minute, to help Véra in the kitchen. I can hear them singing Shri Ram Jai Ram Jai Jai Ram. Some of the potatoes are green inside. I could pretend not to notice. *I could poison all you assholes.* I throw the green potatoes in with the scraps and keep peeling.

Véra touches my hand. "Okay?" she asks.

I will not cry. I will not let her see me cry.

ONE LOOK TOLD me everything.

We were eating lunch, and he waved to someone behind me. I saw the look she gave him before she walked away.

"Who was that?"

"Who?"

"Is that the woman you had that thing with?"

"I didn't have a thing with anyone."

"When you went to Denmark. When you came home crying?"

179

He didn't answer.

"Why did she look at you like that?" *And why is she an older version of me?* "There's something you're not telling me."

"No, lásko."

"So I'm imagining it?"

"No, lásko. But if there's some reason for it then I don't know what it is. She probably felt awkward, because it was very power-ful for her, too."

"Why was it powerful for her?"

"I felt big connection to her. And she's had a depression for the past months."

"You're in contact with her?"

"She text me she have a depression."

"Did you text her back?"

"No."

"So if I look at your texts, I won't see anything from you?" I picked up his phone and found the thread.

> Beloved Parvati. I was so happy to see you are subscribed for the retreat. My beloved Mája is also coming with me there. I wanted to ask you to please do not share with her what we experienced together. It was difficult enough for her the first time. We are very looking forward to be with you soon. Warm and gentle hug, Kuba

"What don't you want her to share with me? What first time?"

"Only what I told you already," he said.

"I know there's more. Don't look at me like that! Tell me what happened."

"Nothing, lásko. Nothing."

I'M PUTTING COOKIES onto a dessert made with quark and bananas. I've been asked to arrange them in the shape of a heart. This is an actual nightmare. He picks up some cookies and tries to help me. His hands are filthy. "Lásko?" he says.

"You know what I'm realising as I make this idiotic dessert?" I scoop out a smear of dirt he's left in the quark. "For the whole time I've known you, I've been trying to make things okay that weren't okay because I thought they were in my head. But they weren't in my head, were they?"

"Lásko moje."

"Can you *please* stop saying that?"

"Will you have a dinner with me?"

"I'm working."

Actually I'm volunteering. I'm volunteering for this.

IT'S POURING RAIN, and he's sitting in the back of the van with a letter in front of him. He asks me to cuddle him. I say, "No, tell me the truth."

"Read the letter," he says.

The letter doesn't say much except that he's sorry, and there's nothing wrong with someone falling in love with him, because he knows how to hold borders.

"So now she's in love with you?"

"I will tell you the truth," he says. "No more lying."

"Make it painful, because that's the only way I'll believe it."

"We experienced quite a deep connection when we met," he says. "But even though I found her attractive, we didn't have anything sexual or we didn't kiss each other. We were talking and sharing a lot, and we, somehow what happened was that, uh, that closeness to her was powerful even though it was clear we will never cross any boundaries because this . . . connection is in the respect towards you and her husband. But I was somehow getting more and more emotional, and I had no control over it. And I felt so sad. I don't know why. And I believe through sharing the depth some very old things opened probably for both of us. I don't know about her. I don't really know her, but I felt so soft and so sad that last few days there I spent crying. It was not connected with her at all. It was somehow my sharing with her made me feel so open and vulnerable, so what I felt was that it was like in the constellations. I don't even have to understand, I probably can't understand, but by allowing those emotions to go through me I'm releasing some pain of my ancestors and who knows who in the lineage who was not able to express the sadness or, I have no idea. I can't explain it logically."

"Why didn't you want her to tell me that?"

"I didn't want you to be disturbed. Because it was fully resolved for me, and I didn't communicate with her for long time. So for me it was closed thing."

"Did you touch her?"

"We hugged."

"That's all?"

"Some of those hugs were quite long."

"Did you tell her how you felt?"

"I don't remember."

"But you told her you had a past life together?"

"I did some shamanic journeys and there was one quite clear one, and I don't remember the details, but what I saw was the little boy being there for his mother instead his father, and I remember I saw clearly that's the pattern what she lives already for many lives. So this meeting what happened to us may improve that for her to not keep happening any more in future. So I asked what action am I supposed to do, and the answer was clear. Let go. Tell her, and then let go."

"So it wasn't romantic?"

"It all felt romantic, but it's romance between son and mother, which I experienced so many times with many others, and I didn't understand it, but I found it so special. I loved to be seen as a man by mothers. I felt like I'm proving the point of myself."

"Great, interesting psychoanalysis, but what I want to know is exactly, physically, what you did with this person."

"A lot of time together. Eye contact. And hug."

"That's it."

"And smoke cigarettes in the forest."

"You told me you were pretending to be a man for her?"

"In the constellation," he says. "I was pretending being her partner, be next to her to show that she can have a strong man next to her."

"Where was her husband during this?"

"At home with her son."

"And that's all?"

"Yes."

"So you won't mind if I check your emails." I open his computer. He doesn't try to stop me. I search for her name and find a long thread. He watches me read it. He calls her *dearest heart* and *half of me* and tells her that what he felt for her was like manna to his soul. She says she has been spending her days dreaming of him, dancing in the nude, and making yoghurt.

He tells her he wants to run to her, but he received a clear message to let her go. She writes back *Ignore that message and come to me! My heart is waiting for you!* After that he suddenly changes. He tells her he knows his place, and it's time to cut it off, for her freedom. She tells him it's terribly painful, but she accepts it.

"Do you want to tell me the truth now?" I ask.

"I can recall that we were not just hugging, but that we were also lying on the mattress holding hands."

"Just hands?"

"Lásko, when I did the ceremony to cut off from her, after I knew that I can never do this kind of things with women again."

"What ceremony?"

"In the forest. After I came home, I ask her to do the ceremony with me, each one in our own forest, and after that it was closed for me."

I ask him to show me how me how he held her. He says no. I lie down. "Show me," I say.

He lies behind me and cups his hands over my abdomen. He kisses my hair and says, "I'm so sorry, lásko."

I turn and face him. "You think you're such a big shaman, but you're just a fucking *liar*."

We're quiet for a while. "What was it about her?" I ask.

"It was deep healing for me," he says. This makes me wild, but I wait for him to finish. "But also I was afraid of her. Like with my mother. She was punishing me when I didn't give her what she wants."

"What did your mother want?"

"She wanted me to be the man for her."

Of course. How predictable. But guess what? My father made me into his little lover, too, and it didn't turn me into a charlatan.

I SHOULD LEAVE, but I can't. Some part of me must want this. I spin lettuce, chop vegetables, arrange butter pats. And I rage. Where does it come from? It keeps boiling and boiling. People give me strange looks, and part of me also watches myself with curiosity. Why am I so angry? What will I do?

The truth keeps coming to me in dreams that wake me up. I shake him, and when he turns toward me blood sprays from his nose onto my face. I wipe it away. I say, "There was no con-stellation, was there? It was just you cuddling and sleeping next to each other."

"Yes."

"And she wasn't the only one, was she?"

"She was the only one I was holding physically," he says. "Mostly I was holding them by invisible strings to their hearts."

"Who?"

"Májenka, all my life I have been living by other people's appreciation. It's my bread and butter. And it's so easy. Especially in the dance world. A few namastes and they're mine. And it's everyone, but there are certain women with same looks, same energy, mostly older ones. Mothers. I always know how to be the best man for them, and I make them sure that if they had me, their life would be perfect, but they can't have me because I was waiting for my goddess. That's you."

Great. Good to know who I am, finally.

He says, "Lásko, I'm so afraid to tell you this . . ."

I'm afraid, too. "Tell me."

"There were others who I was holding physically. It was before I knew you, but I lied about it."

"Who?"

"Šárka."

"You told me you had never been intimate with her."

"It was only physical, and before I know you."

"What difference does that make? The point is you lied."

"I'm sorry, lásko."

"Who else?"

"Solstice."

"What?"

"It was before I know you."

"So *why lie?* Why would it matter?"

"I didn't want you to know how bad it is with me. I was afraid you will run away."

"Who else?"

He hesitates. "Pavla," he says.

"Oh, my God."

"I'm so sorry, lásko."

HE GAVE ME his password. It's Pravda—Truth—with a capital P. My hands are shaking. I type in my own name and find hundreds of messages between me and him. I write *beloved* into the search box. I don't read anything from before we met. I don't need to. And this is only in English. One from some girl named Michelle, whose eyes he would love to see again. From another named Alexa, who is *so special soul,* who he would love to meet to *sing and share together.* From *beloved sister Jennie,* who is still dancing in his heart. From someone named Athena, who was at his concert and felt something move inside when he smiled at her. From Hamida, whose presence is deeply within him. From Sarah, who will never forget the hug he gave her.

When he comes back, he sits on the floor by the door.

"I deleted some other messages today," he says. "It was a folder called slečny. It means ladies. I didn't want that you find it."

So what I read was only what survived his cull.

DURING LUNCH, WE run out of butter. Véra asks me to get more from the freezer in the room that's reserved for the leaders. That woman will be in there, I know it. She's leaving when I arrive. I say, "Are you Parvati?"

She gives me a sad look. She feels sorry for me. I ask if we can talk, and she agrees. She has a posh English accent. We find an empty room upstairs and sit on other people's beds. We're both cross-legged, and she's sitting up very straight, her hands clasped in her lap. Now that we're here, I'm not sure what to say, but she starts.

"In the women's sharing yesterday they were saying how strange it is that Kuba brought his partner and we don't even know her," she says. "They said we should invite you to the circle, but I said no, she has to come to us."

"I'm helping in the kitchen," I say. She looks like she's waiting for me to get to the point. I say, "I wanted to ask you what happened between you and Kuba."

She closes her eyes and takes a deep breath. "When I got Kuba's text asking me not to share with you what is between us, I thought it wasn't very courageous of him."

"What happened between you?"

She holds her hands to her belly. "It was deep healing," she says.

"And what was involved in that?"

"He saw immediately that I am not an ordinary woman," she says.

Oh, right. Ordinary women. Gross.

"I mean what did you do together?"

"We lay together, we slept next to each other, he held me, and it moved some energy that was . . ."

"Was it sexual?"

She looks at me with pity. "It was not about sex," she says. "It was much deeper than that. It was something much, much deeper. But we decided to let each other go. We did a ritual to close it."

"Was what happened between you something you would want your husband doing with another woman?"

"We're divorcing," she says.

"What I mean is, if you were me, knowing what you know, would you want to stay in a relationship with Kuba?"

She closes her eyes, says *hmmm* and shifts from side to side. Then she looks at me and says, "If I was in your position, I would not stay in partnership with him."

I'm sure you'd love that.

I say, "It's not just you, you know? He has lots of women like you. I've participated in one of his letting go ceremonies."

I can tell she's not happy about that, but she maintains her holy pose. She says, "I am not a woman to stand in a queue. If there is even one person in front of me, I will leave."

Well good for you.

"He's very good at getting people hooked on him to feed his diseased ego," I say. "You were just another one of his victims."

"That's your interpretation," she says. She stands and looks down at me. "It's unpleasant to listen to your anger," she says.

"I have to remind myself what is mine and what is yours and give what is yours back to you. But sometimes I feel angry, too. Sometimes I feel like screaming *FUUUUUUUUUUUCK!*"

And she does scream it. Everyone downstairs must hear her. For a second I think I might be wrong about her. I might even like her. But then she pulls herself together and says, "I'm sure you can find someone else. You're beautiful."

I stand up. "Thanks for talking to me," I say. "I'm sorry we couldn't have met under nicer circumstances."

I'M PEELING CARROTS, and he's leading dances. I wonder what those people would think if they knew what their hero is really like. Who am I kidding? They wouldn't care. *That's your interpretation. He was healing her. You're so lucky.*

Someone comes into the kitchen and says, "Come and look at the beautiful princess." I peer out through the glass doors. Parvati is standing under the umbrella I left by the back steps. She's wearing a blue dress with peacock feathers on it and a peacock feather crown. Standing under *my* umbrella! Peacock feathers cascading down her back.

I chuckle at the perfection of this image, and it makes me briefly wonder if Maya, my writer self, is coming back, but she doesn't offer me any passage away from what I feel, so I have to hate Parvati on my own, and with a hatred I can only describe in clichés. I hate her with the fire of a thousand suns. I hate her from the depths of my being. And him. And all of this. They're so sure that they're better than the rest of us in *the outside world.* There is no outside world. It's all in you, you cunts.

SOLSTICE COMES TO sit with me. She's visibly pregnant now and giving me the same look of pity that Parvati gave me. "I wanted to connect with you," she says. "It's hard how Kuba and Tadeáš have so much attention from the women, but you know, last night

I was sitting in the circle, and on all sides of me were former lovers of Tadeáš, and I thought, it's like a family."

I tell her that's not the kind of family I want.

Why don't I leave? Is this what I want? To be right, for once, instead of guilty and wrong?

He goes into the circle, is adored, then comes back to me to be hated. He tells me he's not enjoying any of it. So why doesn't *he* leave? Is this what he wants, too?

I ask him questions, and he answers. Sometimes I shout. Sometimes I cry. Sometimes his nose bleeds. He says his mother used to say he made his nose bleed on purpose to get out of trouble. He tells me he's never loved anyone but me. He tells me this was the soup he was cooked in. It was normal. Lie, cheat, pretend.

"I tried to talk to Tadeáš," he says.

"What did he say?"

"He said, you can't tell them everything."

"Who?"

"Women."

"Wow."

"I told him how I was using my skills as a musician and dance leader to catch people, especially the women. He said, *Yes, but isn't it pleasant to look around the circle and think, I had that one. I had that one. I can have that one.*"

TADEÁŠ STOPS ME in the corridor when I'm on my way to the kitchen. "Beloved one," he says. He puts his hands on my shoulders and kisses my forehead. "I'm glad you are staying," he says. "I know it can be hard sometimes." He doesn't even know me or care who I am. He just doesn't want Kuba to leave.

I say, "I hate lies."

"Yes, but sometimes we don't want to know the *whole* truth," he says. "Do you really want to know the *whole* truth?"

"Actually, I do."

VÉRA TAKES ME aside to sort lettuce. "How are you?" she asks.

"Fine."

"How is it with Kuba?"

"Difficult."

"He doesn't have enough time for you."

Ugh. "It's not that."

I go to the toilet. My period is late again. That woman is here. She shudders when she sees me. *Why the fuck are you shuddering at me? I should be shuddering at you!*

When I get back, Véra asks me how I am again. I say fine, and she says, "Where are you?"

"Thinking."

"You seem to be closed now," she says. "Before you were open. But I love you when you are closed, and I love you when you are open."

I love you too, Véra. You weirdo.

WE HAVE SEX. I need to be close to him. I feel like everything is falling apart. Or it already has, it did a long time ago, but I didn't notice because I had him and all of the distractions that come with him, and I had my signs, which came to fucking nothing, and now I see how fucked up everything is, and he's the only thing left to hold on to. I don't have a calling, I was never guided, and I won't even be able to write about any of this, because who cares? Oh, and I heard it again today. I'm so lucky to be with Kuba. So young and so deep.

I PUT ON my boots and go outside. I don't know where to go. I start to walk to the van, then I turn toward the forest. I feel so lost. I'm crying. He's beside me. I let him hold me. He says, "Please don't leave me, lásko. I never wanted to admit what a liar I am, but I can't continue that way. If you stay, you will have the best husband on the world. I love you so much."

"It's all so stupid," I say. "I thought I came here to grow up somehow, but it's just a repeat of my stupid childhood, and I'm so angry!"

This is what I know. My father the hero off chasing women, my mother at home, miserable and in pain. But which came first? Did he chase women because she was miserable, or was she miserable because he was chasing women? "Oh my God," I say. "I'm becoming her."

"Májenka moje," he says. "If it is in harmony with the universe, I wish for us to grow together all our lives, and I'm asking also for courage to understand and to heal and change together what is broken in us."

SHE'S ALONE, CLEANING something in a bucket. She's just a person, not some devil.

I say, "I'm sorry for being so angry the other day. It was wrong. What I feel has nothing to do with you."

She stands up and wipes her hands on her dress. Imperious, that's the word. She says, "I'm glad you realised that."

IN THE KITCHEN, a woman pulls me aside. "On the first day you were cutting bread, and I came and rearranged it and didn't speak to you," she says. "I'm sorry."

Later, a man sits next to me while I'm eating. "I want to tell you something strange," he says. *Try me.* "I wanted to speak with you sooner, but I am shamed by my English, so now I want only to tell you I like you, and when I see you with Kubík it is so beautiful for me."

When I'm collecting the dishes, I see Kuba sitting with a young woman by the fireplace. His legs are crossed toward her, and his arm is resting along the back of the couch they're both sitting on. I can't believe this is real. I go over to them. He says, "Are you going to dance?" I say no and walk away.

Later he finds me in the kitchen.

"What the fuck is wrong with you?" I say.

"What happened?"

"Are you completely stupid?"

"I am not stupid."

"Did it not occur to you that under the circumstances it might be a good idea to take a little break from adding to your collection?"

"I wanted you to sit on my lap. I wanted to introduce you to her."

"Oh right, you want me to jump on you and say, *He's mine!* Fuck you."

"Lásko, I'm sharing with many people."

"Great! Have fun! Enjoy!" I hit my head. It feels good.

He reaches out, and I slap his hand and walk away. He calls after me. I give him the finger over my shoulder. I don't care who sees this any more. I'm sure they all think I'm a lunatic.

A WOMAN SITS next to me at dinner and says, "I want you to know, I feel you."

"Please tell me what you mean by that," I say.

"I only know there was something between my daughter and Kubík, and it's hard for you."

I have no idea who she is, never mind her daughter. "Thank you for telling me that," I say. "But what's happening between me and Kuba has nothing to do with your daughter."

Later I tell Kuba and point out the woman. He says she's the mother of the person he was sitting with.

"It make a sense," he says. "I was always doing everything to make women feel they are the most special in the world for me, and now they all think they are my special ones."

IN SOME WAYS it's like a nightmare, but it's also like waking up from a nightmare, because at least now I can name the problem instead of being eaten alive by knowing something is wrong but being encouraged—by Kuba, by myself—to ignore it.

Véra tells me about a time when she fell in love with another man at a camp when she and Tadeáš were married, and how that helped her relationship with Tadeáš. Later I see her holding hands with Parvati. I don't know what to think any more. Is there another way to see this?

I tell him I want to leave. I'm going home. I have to say it like I mean it, even though I'm not sure I do and I have no home to go to.

"Please, lásko," he says. I walk away from him. He takes a few steps after me and falls on his knees. He puts his face on the floor. I leave him to it.

I DON'T SAY goodbye to anyone except Véra. I fall asleep in the van so I don't have to witness Kuba's goodbyes to all those vampires.

We arrive at night and go straight to bed. In the morning, I wake up before him and climb down the ladder. I sit at the altar and try to meditate, but I can't. I put my face into my heart pillow and cry myself back to sleep.

I SKYPE WITH Becca. I left my computer in the van, so I use Kuba's. She tells me that Drew has a new girlfriend, a German biologist slash marathon runner. I ask what she's like, and Becca says, "She's not you," which means she likes her. They're probably friends. I'm happy for him. He deserves to be happy.

I tell her about Kuba's women, a short version. She would never say she told me so. "Come home," she says. "I'll buy you a ticket. Or I can buy you a ticket to New Zealand if that's what you want. But please don't stay there."

It's the same advice I would give to someone in my position— get the hell out of there. But I'm bound to him somehow. When

I consider the possibility that I will never get to sleep by a camp-fire with him again, that he will never sing me Kometa again, it's unbearable. And what if he changes? If I leave now, I will have gone through this for someone else's benefit, let him climb on my back on his way to heaven.

His email browser is open, so I search for my own name. All of the results are either to or about me. I try lásko. It's still mostly me. Then, two pages in, I find his other Mája. I climb the ladder and shake his leg.

He starts at the beginning. At first it's transparent but harm-less flirtation. She talks about her experiences with tantra and a retreat where she was alone in the dark for a week and all of the amazing insights she had. They start to develop inside jokes. She sends him a poem she wrote about him. They never men-tion me or her partner or why they're writing to each other in the middle of the night.

Eventually he tells her about his vision of life in South Bohemia with the wife and children and thyme tea. He tells her that his beloved Májenka doesn't want to live in the Czech Republic, and it's hard for him. He says he found himself look-ing at her *magnificent* profile picture again and again, and he's confused. She and I are like copies of each other, and he's not sure which one is real.

She tells him they are from the same soul family, but she doesn't know if they will be able to be together in this life. He says he wants to meet her, then he says what they're doing is wrong and he doesn't want to communicate any more, then he writes that he would not have let me come to the Czech Republic if he had thought there was a chance for him to be with her. He agrees to meet her, then he tells her he can't meet her. He's with me. He loves me.

I smash my frame drum over the cherub head bookend, then I pick up the head and throw it down from the loft. It explodes on the floor. I climb down the ladder, pull a photograph off the wall and rip it in half. I reach for the one of Kuba rowing across the Ganges. "Please, lásko, don't," he says. I rip it twice and drop the pieces onto the ground, then I go to his altar and swipe everything off onto the floor. He jumps down from the loft and holds me from behind, pinning my arms to my sides. "Stop!" he shouts.

"Or what?"

He lets me go. I take the framed drawing from his altar and smash the glass against the edge of the table. I take out the picture. Behind it is the photograph of him and Pavla staring into each other's eyes. He looks surprised, but I'm not. I rip both pictures in half. I pull down a bundle of feathers hanging from the ceiling, and he grabs me again and holds my hands behind my back. "Be careful!" he says.

I laugh. "What are you going to do to me?"

"It's not about me," he says.

"Ooh, are the *bird* spirits going to get me?"

He picks me up, pushes me outside the door, and leans against it. When he lets me back in, I take his owl wing down from where it's hanging by the door. He tries to pry open my hands.

"Please," he says. "This room is the only thing in the world that is keeping me with any sanity."

"These things are not real!" I scream. I let go of the wing and move on to breaking other things. I can hear him breathing behind me. I turn around. He reaches into his back pocket and pulls out his knife. We watch each other as he opens it, then he takes a painting from his dresser, stabs it and drags the knife through it. I pick up the angel ornament Sophie gave us and rip off its wings. Orange flakes scatter everywhere.

We work together until everything that can be broken is broken, then we lie on the floor. The cherub dust is everywhere. God knows what's in it.

I tell him my period is late.

"Is it true, love?"

"I'm not pregnant, if that's what you're thinking. This is what happens if I get too stressed. You start bleeding, I stop."

I sit in the hammock and he rolls me a cigarette. He says the hardest thing is imagining me being happy with someone else when it was supposed to be him. "I planned a boat trip for you, and there were so many surprises prepared," he says. "It was going to be such a special time. If you stay, I'm ready to leave everything, Májenka. I built such a mess here, but I don't want to live this way any more. And I'm sad about some of the things we broke, but I'm also relieved, because I want to start from the zero."

GINA SAYS THAT ignorant people are avatars of the Buddha who appear in our lives to help us burn off bad karma. I tried to imagine the other Mája that way, and it was sort of helpful. Then I tried it with Parvati, and I got so angry I hung up on Gina.

Parvati wrote to him. She said she was angry after I hurled my jealousy at her, but she wants him to know that she forgives him.

"I wasn't jealous," I say. "I was outraged. It's like calling me greedy because I don't want someone eating off *my* plate."

"She is totally out of the sense," he says.

"You know she told me I should leave you?"

"At the retreat she was still hunting me," he says. "She was still playing the game even then. And I told her I want to apologise . . ."

"At the retreat?"

"Yes. I went to her to close it properly. I said I want to apologise, and she said that's good that I apologise, and she will not give me anything any more."

"What did you say?"

"I told her that's right."

I have no energy to talk. I fall asleep on the floor. He joins me, and when I wake up, I'm raging again. I shake him, and he says, "Please, lásko. I can't continue. I'm too tired." I ask him if he told anyone else about his other Mája. He says he told Ondra.

"What did you tell him?"

"I showed him her picture and told him how I am confused."

"What did he say?"

"Ty jsi tak božská žena."

"Answer the fucking question, Kuba."

"He said she is like you, and he said he cross fingers for me."

I go to the toilet. When I come back, I tell him I have my period, and we make love among the broken bits of cherub head. It's all falling apart. Both of our computers have stopped working. There's blood on the bed, and the blankets are filthy. He says, "Soon the house will fall onto the van, and we will be standing naked on the garden with big crater where the house was, and we will say, *Hey, let's make love.*"

I DREAMT THAT Kuba gave me a piece of yellowed cloth. I unfolded it and saw it was the handkerchief my mother gave me, but it was embroidered with a duck instead of a cross and a quote from the Bible. I understood that he knew where she was, or how to reach her. I said, "Please let me see her," but he shook his head. "Then show me your real face." I knew as I said it that I had made his mask and I could take it off. I stepped toward him and did a motion with my hand, and behind his beautiful face I saw a small, grey being like the ones in my nightmares.

VÉRA LEFT ME several messages, so I called her back and told her everything. I assumed she'd be sympathetic, but she just said, "Make up your mind. Stay with him or don't." As if she didn't know from experience that it's not that simple.

He's had a headache for three days. I actually feel good, physically. Better than I have in a long time. And I look good. It's so weird. My eyes are clear. My skin glows. My tongue feels . . . normal. No shaking walls. Emotionally, I'm all over the place. When he sings to me, I get sucked in, but then I think about his lies, and his other Mája, and him sleeping with his arms around that woman . . . whatever. This is reality. He's not Nohavica. Even Nohavica isn't Nohavica. He isn't Kometa. He just sings it.

KUBA IS ASLEEP in his sleeping bag by the altar, and I'm in the loft looking through his Facebook friends. I'm going to go through every single person until I find his other Mája. It doesn't take long. She works at a vegetarian restaurant in the city centre. She's written a non-fiction book about her travels in Japan. I click on her *magnificent* profile picture. I click through to see more. There are so many, and in every one she has this same coy expression, like *I'm so cute and sweet and innocent.* Is she pretty? She is. I hate that she is.

It's too painful to keep looking at her, imagining him looking at her, so I open his Facebook messages and search for her profile name. I find an epic thread. I copy and paste some of it into the translator. It's much more painful than the pictures. And he was writing her those things while he and I were on our bike trip. How can that be? I thought we were so happy.

I look at her pictures again. Every one makes me hate her more. Then I find the worst one. It's black and white. She's lying on the grass with her fist under her chin like a Sears model. Behind her arm I can see a black cord around her neck, and nestled into the notch at the base of her throat are two conjoined crystals.

I take off my necklace and hurl it at the sink. It hits the curtain. That won't do. There's a glass of water next to me. I throw it at the door, and it shatters.

Kuba yelps. He must have been sleeping.

"You gave her my crystals!"

"What?"

"I saw your other Mája wearing them. On Facebook."

He comes out from under the loft. "Not your one," he says. He looks ill. His skin is grey, and there's dried blood around his nostrils. "I have more of them that looks same."

Of course. A collection.

I put on my flip flops and walk past the broken glass. I'm going to have a shower. At least the water pressure is good in this hellhole.

I automatically hold down the handle before I close the door. I let it go and slam the door, open it and slam it again and again. I gave myself up, learned nothing, grew . . . not at all. I'm just a hateful goblin in this awful house.

The *Become a Buddha* sign is gone from the shower basin, but the ladder is still there. I sit down and let the water fall on my back as I cry. I wish I could be the next woman Kuba loves. The younger one, the Czech one, the more free, more spiritual one. Then again, I'm not her, and I can't be her, and I would rather be me.

EVERY BOOK I pick up, every song Kuba translates, seems to be about me, not in a way that makes me feel less alone, but in a way that makes me feel like an automaton running a programme that's been run billions of times before.

I'm re-reading *The Unbearable Lightness of Being*. I wish I'd done it before I came to this country. I might have saved myself the trouble. I'm playing Tereza, the unmothered book-worm, and Kuba is playing Tomas, the inveterate philanderer who she offered herself to, sick and helpless. Together we've surrendered our fates to fortuities, discovering too late that we walked into a trap, because the events of our lives aren't meant to be, they just are.

Once when Kuba was leading a dance at some event I was reminded of Tereza's dream about being forced to sing and march naked with other women while Tomas shouted orders from above. What I forgot about her dream was that Tomas was shooting the women if they didn't follow his orders perfectly, and with the exception of Tereza, the women were delighted to obey him. I also forgot Tereza's conclusion about the dream's meaning, or at least my understanding of her conclusion—that Tomas didn't see a difference between her body and other women's bodies. To him, her body, and the soul it housed, weren't special, which was, pathetically, what she wanted most. By refusing to allow her that, he had condemned her to worthlessness, delivered her back to her indifferent mother.

"I'm afraid you will leave me," he says.

"You could be with your other Mája then. You love her."

"I don't love her. I don't mean to be proud, but if I want her, I am with her now. I wanted to not lose my country and not lose you. I wanted you in Czech Republic."

"You made me sick. You wanted to keep your collection, and your lies, and you didn't care if it made me die or go insane."

"I didn't know what you feel! Now is first time what I know what is happening in you. You never showed me nothing!"

"How could I?"

"My love, we have the same fears. But I wish you to see that I was a true as my braveness allowed, and I think it was same for you."

"So you don't love her?"

"To be honest, I believe truthfully shared story makes you love anyone. It's what I love on dance camps. We are singing about things what everyone can relate to like pain, transformation, forgiveness, and we are opening the space to see in each person's eyes the mirror of own soul."

How dare he teach me? I want to love and forgive everyone too, but I can't because I feel attacked all the time, and it's his fault! But there's still doubt. Am I missing the bigger picture?

I don't know. What I do know is that real life will never begin. Everything will continue to be incomplete and unsatisfying—a provizorium, as Kuba would say—and I should be grateful to be dealing with such petty disappointments. I should be grateful.

WE CAME TO Kampa Island for a music workshop, but I felt too uncomfortable to stay, so I'm walking across Charles Bridge. It might be the last time. I try to feel nostalgic, but there are so many tourists with iPhones.

I'm standing under the tower arch when I have a thrilling, awful idea. I take out my phone and check Google Maps. The café where the other Mája works is a three-minute walk from here.

I wonder if she'll recognise me. She might have searched for me online, but my Facebook profile picture is a *New Yorker* cartoon, and I write under a pseudonym. It's possible that Kuba's showed her a picture of me or she's seen me at an event. Even if she does recognise me, I doubt she'll let on unless I bring it up. Will I bring it up? I don't even know if she speaks English. She works in food service in Prague 1, though, so she must at least be conversant.

The restaurant is down a cobblestoned side street. Inside, a waiter greets me. I ask for a table for one, and I try not to be obvious about looking around as he leads me past the bar into a dark blue room and points to a table next to a stone fireplace. There's a book on one of the chairs.

The English name of the restaurant is Clear Head. The logo is a flying head with wings, and the ceiling is painted as a galaxy with pinpoints of light coming through as stars. Behind me is an illuminated display of religious symbols and the faces of saints and sages. Ram Dass is there, laughing.

I order a green juice and a pot of jasmine tea. While I'm waiting, I brace myself for her to walk through the doorway, but she doesn't. The waiter brings my drinks. I pick up the book on the chair across from me. It's in English. It's called *Zen Heart, Zen Mind*. I open it to a random page and read:

> *Realize you are emptiness, openness, oneness.*
> *That is what your mind and heart are. Just be*
> *that. Not so much in total clarity and purity,*
> *but in darkness and unknowing, from where*
> *arise transcendental faith and trust and love.*

The name of the restaurant, the logo, the stars, the laughing Ram Dass, the quote—moments like this make me believe that the universe is also playful, not only holding our feet to the flames.

On my way out, I notice one of Kuba's posters on the message board by the door. His legs are crossed under and around his sitar, and his head is tucked and turned to one side, like a horse whose rider is drawing back on its reins. Next to his poster is a smaller flyer featuring the other Mája. It's an advertisement for her book launch. Her hand is under her chin, knuckles up, like in a graduation portrait, and she wears the same expression I've seen in so many of her photos online, a kind of guileful imitation of innocence. Or maybe that's wrong. I don't know what's going on in her head. I only know about myself, because I've played the same game, albeit in different ways. Less obviously, I'd like to think, but not because I'm less vain. My pose is refusing to pose. My strategy is preemptive retreat, not because I hate to lose or don't care about winning, but because I'm afraid that if people see me, they will hurt me. She has her own strategies, no doubt, and her own reasons for having them, but neither of us invented this game. Nor did Kuba.

For goodness' sake, the only reason I care about this so much is because it's happening to me. When I read Kundera's novel, I don't hate Tomas for cheating on Tereza, and I don't hate the women he cheats on her with. They're just characters in a story.

KUBA IS PACKING his instruments when I come back, so I sit with Claire, the French therapist from camp. She asks me how I am, and I tell her a short version of the truth. She says she knew he had those problems in the past, with Liliana, but she's sorry to hear it's happening with me, because it seemed like he had changed and we were meant for each other.

"I want to apologise," she says.

"Why?"

"Because we were all saying why is Kubík with you? We said, she's so lucky, she should be happy, but she seems to be so unfriendly and strange, and he can have any woman."

I thank her. It's a relief to know that what I felt was real. Then she tells me about how she and Kuba knew each other in a past life but they can't be together in this life, and I nod.

On the drive home, I tell him I had a moment today when I could see things differently.

"What it means?" he asks.

"I mean sometimes I think I created this whole situation."

"We created it both," he says, and for now, at least, I agree.

I HAVE AN idea. It came to me this morning in the kind of all-at-once flash of inspiration I haven't had for ages. A woman named Maya goes to the Czech Republic to find out about her roots. She's housesitting this decrepit mansion in South Bohemia, and worrying that the neighbouring farmer is going to rape her, and trying to decide if she should visit this charismatic Czech guy she's been communicating with online. She wakes up one night, and she's paralysed. There's a light burning through her window, and there's a small, grey being standing at the end of her bed. She's lifted through the window on the beam of light and taken to a spaceship where this otherworldly man with white-blonde hair and blue eyes speaks to her telepathically and tells her not to be afraid. Then, like in those alien abduction narratives, he brings her to a half-human, half-alien baby and forces her, like through eye contact he can control her, to hold it to her breasts, which, to her horror, are leaking milk. She wakes up back in the farmhouse, and she remembers a dream with different but parallel details to the abduction—so tractor beams shining through the window, the farmer at the end of her bed. At first it seems like the abduction was a nightmare, but from that point on the story is split between her in captivity in the spaceship—where she becomes obsessed with the white-blonde man and believes she is volunteering to take care of the baby, thereby serving a benevolent alien society that will save humanity from itself—and her experiences in the Czech Republic, where she's falling in love with this guy and trying to fit into his crazy life but also sensing something is very wrong. The two realities cross-over through her dreams and the visions and synchronicities she experiences, then start to merge after a disturbing discovery, which in the Czech world would be that her guy is a liar and in the spaceship world would be that the baby she's taking care of is her own, and she's been an abductee used for breeding purposes since her adolescence but had her memories erased. She tries to escape with the baby, and in the process she comes to understand the greater goals of the aliens, which obviously don't centre human ideas of good and evil, and to accept that she was, after all, a volunteer. She decides to forget again and go back to her life on earth with the understanding that no one is coming to save us, we're responsible for ourselves and each other, and when she says goodbye to the white-blonde man she sees him as he truly is, the small, grey alien from the beginning of the story. Back on earth, she and her Czech guy are in Varanasi, and he proposes to her at the burning ghat. She gives a noncommittal answer, and on her way back to the guesthouse she passes a man with white-blonde hair and has the overwhelming feeling that she knows him. She stumbles, and he catches her, and, even though she knows it's totally corny, she says, "I know you," and that's the end. The relationship between the two plots would be left up to interpretation, so either plot could be written by the Maya of either reality, or both could be happening simultaneously in parallel realities, or the abduction plot could represent Maya's unconscious experience, or it's possible the abduction story is real and the other story is a screen memory implanted to account for the traces of erased memories and feelings (and maybe scars?) from repeat abductions, or either the real-life story or the abduction story could represent the ways people disconnect from themselves through spiritual practices, intoxicants, infatuation, denial, dissociation, even creativity. I feel excited about this idea!

I'VE GONE OFF that book idea. I can't write about aliens.

It's his birthday. We're in the forest. He's made a fire on the rock where we called our ancestors. He asks if I trust him.

"Of course not."

"It's visible."

"What did you expect? You were lying to me the whole time."

"Nothing what I did takes away from my love to you. Do you believe that?"

"No."

"I was afraid, Májenka. I didn't want to lose my home."

"Do you really think you have some soul connection with all those women?"

"Who?"

"Barbora, Parvati, that other Mája . . ."

"I wanted it to look like that. I made up so many things. I don't know."

"Be honest. Do you think you were from the same soul family or whatever?"

"When I met that other Mája, I was so strong man on the mission. Every single bird poo falling onto the ground made sense to

me, everything was guiding me, and she was impressed by how
I was cool, and after she wrote me some text and expressed some
appreciation, and it started a fire. But she was the one who was telling me how we are connected on a soul level and from the past life."

"You know what bothers me most? If people could admit that
they were being selfish jerks I would be like fine, I get it. It's the
way you all pretend it's some holy destiny."

"You don't understand the basic," he says. "It's the need to be
not wrong, to be good, to not be blamed. So if I see I did a mistake,
I say, *No it's totally pure! It's the spiritual love!* That's automatic
reaction. To shape the reality different way. Can you understand it?"

"I hear what you're saying."

He uses his owl wing to fan the flames. "I thought you were
supposed to give that to the place where you wanted to put the
bus," I say.

He keeps fanning. "It got a different purpose now."

"What's that?"

"I don't know. But I can see we will not live the visions what
I had."

"How do you feel about that?"

"I'm grieving, because I liked that vision and the way how
it appeared."

"Is there a but? Or just the grieving."

"Also accepting. And accepting myself, also. Because I didn't
stop loving myself, Májenka. I did so stupid things, and I saw
what I was doing, and I said okay, so this is still part of me. I'm
going to face it."

He puts down the wing and sits next to me. "I have to tell you
something," he says. Oh God. What now? "I panicked. I wanted
you to be friends, so I lied."

"About what?"

"I had something with Véra. Before I knew you."

I flash through every interaction I've seen him have with her.

"Why would you lie? What does it matter if you were with her before you knew me?"

He sighs. "After she came for my drum workshop what you stayed home for, she was writing me how hard it is for her that I didn't touch her, how she is missing it."

"And how did you answer?" He gets out his phone and finds the message. He tells her the connection is so strong, and they both know it, but he has to hold borders to respect his relation-ship with me.

"It has to be fucking hard being my partner," he says.

I say, "It doesn't have to be, but it is."

GOD, IT'S SO obvious. I did the same thing. I didn't lie about it, but I did the same thing. Much worse, actually.

It was at a writer's retreat. He claimed he was in an open marriage. By the time he'd admitted that wasn't true, it was too late. I told myself it wasn't real life. On my way home I ate a double bacon cheeseburger at the airport to prove to myself that I wasn't who I thought I was. Who I was pretending to be.

I told Drew, and he hooked up with someone at a confer-ence to get back at me. I didn't care. That's when I knew it was over. He was in Toronto, and he called me from his hotel room as soon as she left. He was distraught. I had to talk him down. I really didn't care.

THERE'S A PAVED path down to the Vltava. Kuba says he remem-bers when it was dirt, but now the cement looks ancient. He takes off all his clothes and dips himself into the cold water from a pushup position, like it's his lover.

"What are you thinking?" he asks when he comes out, drip-ping and gorgeous.

I was thinking about how I'll laugh about all of this one day with my future husband, who would never lie to me.

"I've invented a new religion," I say. "It's called shut up and meditate. But I don't know how to meditate, so it's just called shut up."

"I'm your devotee," he says.

I tell him to shut up.

On the way back to the van, he shows me the circle of trees where he and Ondra and their friend who died had their final meeting.

"He was so lovely," Kuba says. "Him and Ondra. I always felt like I'm so bad next to them. I was the cheater and liar, and they were living integrity. They were such good boys."

KUBA IS VISITING Otto in the hospital. When he gets home, I'm on the floor reading *The Unbearable Lightness of Being*. My robe is up around my thighs.

He says, "Hello, lásko." I don't answer. He brings the rest of his stuff inside and closes the door.

"Do you want tea?" he asks.

He kneels behind me and kisses the backs of my legs. He lifts my robe, strokes me, bites me gently. I pretend to ignore him and reread the same sentence again and again.

"Good book?" he says. He looks at the cover. "The one with sex in mirrors?" Of course that's what he would remember.

He picks up his guitar, leans against the wall, and plays a song. I ask him what it's about. "It's about how difficult it is to walk through life," he says. "Sometimes you feel like giving up, because you haven't finished grieving for one thing, and the next one is already lining up."

The sun is shining on me, and I feel warm and calm. "I'm having a happy moment," I say.

"Heavy?"

"Happy."

"You are sweetheart," he says. "We should stick together."

ANOTHER DANCE RETREAT. I shouldn't be here, but being at home imagining it would be so much worse.

He says he's going to take a break from being a leader, but he'd already committed to this retreat. I know the real reason he had to come. There's a bigshot American leader here, and Kuba doesn't want to miss an opportunity to be close to someone famous. I also know that she's invited him to come to the States, and he's more or less agreed to go, but he hasn't told me yet. Maybe he thinks he doesn't have to inform me about things any more now that I have his email password.

When he comes back, he says the usual things. I'm his little animal. His hummingbird. He loves me so much. He's so good at creating feelings of devotion. He only has to play the opening chords of Přijdu hned and I'm his.

HE FINALLY TELLS me about his plan to go to the States. He says they will pay for his ticket and part of mine if I join him. I won't stop him from going, but I won't go with him. I'll go to New Zealand instead.

I'm reading his emails again. It's so toxic, but I can't stop. I translate every message—it's a painful way to learn a language, but effective. Not all of them need to be translated. A girl named Gemma writes him that he is in her heart, and she is so happy to know he exists. He responds:

> Dear Gemma, I want to share something with you. In the past, I was writing you things like you are beautiful and we have so special connection. I am learning that this is not the best way to communicate, because it can cause a misunderstanding. And I want to tell you that for me our relationship is just a friendship. Looking forward to seeing you soon on New Mexico!

So she'll be there. Is she the reason he's going? She writes back almost immediately. She says it is much more than friendship, they are soul lovers, and soon she will be able to tell him that while they are looking into each other's eyes.

From the rest of his messages I gather that he's planning more and more events, workshops, a silent retreat. And of course there are more women. It's like whac-a-mole. He writes them to apologise and cut off contact, but he can't leave it at that, he has to explain the process he's going through, his *transformation*, and they lap that shit up. They write things like, "Oh, what a beautiful soul you are. I would love to have tea with you to share more." One of them writes him about ten responses in the first twenty-four hours. The final one is novella-length, with the subject "One Last Thing." She tells him he is the most important person in her life, even more than her husband and children. She says she has never felt what she felt with him before, and nothing can make her doubt that it was real.

The only outlier is Véra. Her response to his long email declaring his regret and determination to change amid thinly-disguised blame and justification is one sentence, in English: "Why don't you take a break before you start carving a golden statue of Jakub the Integrated Man."

I'VE BOUGHT A ticket. I have to get away from him, because when I'm with him I don't know my own mind. I told Gina I'll be a mess when I arrive, and she said, "When you get here we have to celebrate my birthday, because I don't know how many I have left."

I'm crying all the time. I can't get to Penny Market and back without stopping to cry. I still want to change all of this somehow. The image of Kuba with someone else, me alone. Now I will be old again. Another broken heart in a world full of broken hearts.

I PLAN TO tell him I'm leaving as soon as he comes through the door. Instead I say, "You should go to New Mexico."

"If I don't go there, I feel it's against me," he says. "But if I do go there, I feel it is against you."

"So go." He smiles. He's totally misreading this. He sits next to me on the bed and takes my hand.

"You are amazing," he says.

"I'm leaving."

"Where?"

"New Zealand."

"I will come with you," he says.

"Don't you ever feel angry for my sake?" I ask. "Like what am I to all these women? Nothing. Garbage. Does that matter to you?"

"I'm sorry about your experiences with me," he says. "But I don't feel so guilty any more, because I understand myself better, and I see that you were also the faker, and you were also selfish."

"How was *I* selfish?"

"I didn't mean it so literally."

"Was it a metaphor?"

"No, but I meant I don't see you so angelic as I used to."

"Do you want to explain to me how it's my fault that you were chasing every skirt that crossed your path because, what, I was wearing makeup?"

"That's not what I said."

"It's *exactly* what you said . . ."

"No, you are putting the words into my mouth."

"I am listening to the words coming out of your mouth."

"You are not."

"So explain. What did you mean when you called me selfish?"

"It's big struggle for me when I'm trying to express my support to you and you jump into my sentence."

"Fine, I won't jump in. What did you mean?"

"It's not about blaming. I was describing how our mechanisms were encouraging each other. You were acting from your need of security, and I was acting from mine. You were manipulating me as I was manipulating you. And we created this both. Like you said before that you were afraid one day you will realise you were creating this all."

"Wouldn't that be convenient, if I decided it was my fault? Because as a *spiritual* person, and especially as a spiritual *woman*, I should suck it up and be grateful, right? And if I can't, if I'm very, very *angry* or if it makes me *sick*, well that's a big failure."

"When you are like this I feel like the mouse with the elephant," he says. "It's scary, but on the other hand I understand your emotions, and I understand that it's difficult for you to stop once you started."

I break the teapot, and he leaves. I try to stop him. I tell him I'll break everything in the room, but he ignores me. I feel so, so bad. I want to get out of my skin. I want to scream or run into the street. This isn't my life. That's what I keep telling myself. But what is? What is even real?

I hate myself. And I hate my stupid, unfinishable novel. And my other novel, too. It's mean-spirited and moralising. Every time I wrote anything heartfelt I had to acknowledge every possible objection or undermine it with some dismissive aside, because I wouldn't want to be accused of trying to humanise my awful protagonist, who I made as unlike me as possible and spent the entire book attacking with dramatic irony to maximise the distance between us.

When Kuba comes back, he holds me, and I cry. He tells me he won't go to the States. He says he loves all my parts. "I'm not giving up," he says. "I still think we are not lost. I never made any effort for anyone if I compare to what I'm doing for our relationship, even though it probably doesn't seem like it sometimes. And I will never leave you. You are the only one I want to stay with. I love you more than my family, because you are my family. I love you more than myself, because you are myself."

It's what I want to hear, but it doesn't reach my heart. It's just words. He pours them into me, and I feel better, but it doesn't change anything.

OTTO DIED. KUBA goes to the forest, and he's gone all night. In the morning, I take the train to Prague and visit the church behind Václavské náměstí where he brought me once. Then I walk to the Museum of Communism and sit with a couple in a dark room to watch a documentary about the demonstrations on the twentieth anniversary of Jan Palach's self-immolation. Over images of people being beaten and tear-gassed by the police, a song plays, with subtitles.

God created a twig
For me to make wreaths.
Thank you for the pain
That teaches me to ask questions.
Thank you for the failure
That makes me work hard
To be able to bring a gift
Even if no strength is left.

Thank you, thank you.

I let myself cry without trying to sort out why, or who for, because all pain is a palimpsest—written, effaced, overwritten, until we can't hope to understand, we can only feel it.

When the film is over, I wait for the couple to leave. The woman squeezes my shoulder as she passes behind me.

At home, Kuba is lying in the garden. I lie next to him. "Otto's spirit visited me at night," he says.

"And?"

"I asked him how it is. He said it's very different from what we guessed."

I take his hand. "I was looking at the stars just now," he says. "And I thought, we are just the souls on the training, and we helped each other so much."

WE'RE AT ANOTHER ayahuasca ceremony, for two nights this time. Eliáš is here, the guy who telepathically told me off after I telepathically hit on him. I avoid him completely.

We set up our beds. I've decided to be in a different room from Kuba. I want to be alone.

There's a woman named Kateřina here. Kuba told me she was at some event he did recently, and since then she's been writing to him that she's so strongly attracted to him and blah, blah, blah. No matter where we go, there's always at least one.

I forgot my heart-shaped pillow in the van. I go to get it and meet Pavla in the driveway. I keep walking. I won't let her disturb me.

I get my pillow and walk back toward the house. Kuba and that Kateřina are in the gazebo in the back yard. They are sitting cross-legged on the ground and seem to be deep in conversation. I am totally fed up with this nonsense.

I tell him I have to talk to him and walk away without acknowledging her. He follows me into the house.

"What were you doing with that woman?"

"She ask me . . ."

"You know what you're doing."

"Do you want to leave, lásko?"

"I want you to *stop!*" He looks at me helplessly. "Pavla's here," I say.

"She is also coming for these ceremonies once upon a time."

"It's now and then!"

"Do you want to leave, lásko?" he asks. I ignore him. I came here for myself, and I will not be disturbed by these fools.

We're called into the ceremony room for a meeting. Pavla is in the farthest corner away from Kuba, and Kateřina is setting up her bed next to him. All of her actions seem deliberately sensual. She arranges her bedding as if she was performing the dance of the seven veils. During the sharing, she moans approvingly and bows to each person after they speak. When it's her turn, she talks forever. Pavla doesn't say anything. I just say my name.

Dante gives me much more than last time, and I drink it all. Then I sit in my place and wait.

The first thing is flowers blooming like a symphony. Huge orange lilies, then hundreds of small, colourful flowers. They bloom faster and faster as the view pulls out and crescendos in a giant lotus. I think I'm going to throw up, but instead I yawn. I feel a pulsing blue light around my body. My head falls back, and the light pours into me through my mouth. I travel up it, as if I'm moving through a tube toward the sun. There is so much energy behind me, but I can't get there. I'm blocked. *Discipline is a balance of will and surrender. You're trying to colonise your heart with your head. Surrender to your heart.*

There's water dripping. The guy next to me vomits. I see four teenagers riding old-fashioned bikes over a bridge in sepia light. They're laughing. *There doesn't always have to be a dark side.* I'm inside something and moving up and out again. My head falls back. *You're always trying to control your experience. Open up. Open up to everything.* I inwardly agree, and I expect to spill out into the cosmos, but instead I'm besieged by a nightmarish maelstrom of images. I manage to get my bucket in time to vomit into it before I am cast into this hellish tornado, which accelerates, spinning and multiplying until it dissolves into a vacuum where there's nothing to hold onto, nothing to identify with. I try to go back, because the vacuum is so much worse than the tornado.

Another vision appears. A boy is by a fence. He wants to climb over, but he can't because he's too small. The guy next to me is vomiting again. The water is still dripping. The boy tries to crawl under the fence, but he's too big. It's a parable. Yes. It's about. It's about . . . It means . . . *Bullshit!* Something rips the vision away. Oh no, I know this. I've been through all of this before. Someone laughs. Someone moans orgasmically. She says, "Vodu?" The water is dripping in a pattern. There's a message in it. No there isn't. I know that, I know what it's like to almost understand it, and I know what it's like to have it ripped away by that . . . claw?

Okay, a crocodile. No, I know this. I will stop it by thinking about something else. What about my book? Should I include the aliens? *Bullshit!* Ugh. That's so mean! Sebastian is tending to the guy next to me. The guy is crying a lot and saying, "Prosím!"

I see myself caressing Kuba's face and sighing. *Bullshit!* The claw snatches him away. Oh, stop it, stop it! The sounds in the room are following my visions. Someone laughs. Someone moans orgasmically. She says, "Vodu?"

Sebastian says, "No." Everyone laughs. Why are they laughing at her? That's awful.

"I can't do that," she says in English. "No. That's not for me. That's enough. Sebastian, I want to go to the toilet. Not now. Sebastian? I want to go to the toilet. Not *now!* I don't want to go now! Sebastian?"

"Do you want to go to the toilet?"

"Yes," she says. "Yes, no, yes, no, yes, no, yes and no." Everyone laughs, but it's so sinister, because I think they're all trapped in this too, and their laughter is involuntary.

I see my parents' bed. My mother's side is empty. It's the middle of the night, and I've had a nightmare. I find her sitting at the kitchen table in her nightgown. Her bare feet are dirty, her hair is hanging down over her face. I see an old woman who I know is my grandmother. She's sitting outside of a pub, counting money on a table. *You don't have to judge this.* Okay, let's just say someone did something bad. *You don't have to judge it.* Let's say something bad happened. *You don't have to judge it.* Maybe she was waiting there to protect my mother. *You don't have to judge it.*

My head falls back. I see the stars. There are a million gears working my brain in different directions. Another image slots into view. Swinging doors like in a saloon, and in the middle a laughing neon green clown face. If I see what's on the other side of those doors, I will understand. But I have to go through the clown face to get there, and I will not. I have to, though. I will. I will. I move forward. Now there are millions of clown faces going up and down like a slot machine. If I go through there, will I come out on the other side? Will I still be me? *There's only one way to find out.* I'm so afraid. I move closer, and the view pulls back, the clown faces are a detail on the skirt of a woman stenciled in light, floating in empty space. There's a terrifying *WHOMP* sound as I'm sucked between her legs, drawn into a gaping emptiness, and . . . NO!

Something pushes my head into my bucket, and snakes lunge at me as I vomit. *You were told what to do, and you didn't do it. Why are you here?* I'm sorry. I understand now. I lie down. I feel good, or better. The visions are gone. It's over. Never again. I will never do this again. I have to remember. Do not do this again.

THERE'S A FIELD across the road and a grove of trees and some mountains in the distance. I hum the national hymn to myself. *Where is my home? Where is my home?* My mother used to sing me to sleep with it. She stroked my hair. Kuba does that.

He sits next to me. I ask him what happened. "I was on the toilet, and aliens were scanning my body," he says. "Then I saw the Czech Christmas. It's the cosiest thing. It make a sense. It's so tidy. But what is it? We eat carp and potato salad and have a

Christmas tree and sing about the shepherds who see the falling star, but we imagined it happened in Beskydy Mountains in two metres of snow. I felt like it's so confusing. It's all so confusing . . . Because it's not real. It's important, but it's not real. It's important to get over it. And, I don't know. It was so safe."

"I'm sorry," I say.

"Why?"

"I'm so judgmental."

"Májenka, if it wasn't for your judgments, I would never change myself."

"Sometimes I think people hate me," I say. "Or they would if they knew me."

"Sweetheart, it's mainstream feeling," he says. "But I believe if we are not ignorant we would not be on this planet."

I tell him I'm going to be in the van during the next ceremony. I can't go back in there after what happened last night.

"Did you talk to Pavla?" I ask.

"Can I tell you one story?"

"Okay."

"Close from our house is one old woman, and once upon a time I help her with the things like to carry something heavy or stack the firewood. Once I was asking Otto to help me help her with something what was too much for me, and he did it, but he was not happy about it. So I ask him what's the problem, and he told me during the communism she was reporting his family to the secret police and because of that his father lost his job and he was kicked off from the university. But he still have to live nearby her and treat her like the human being. And with Pavla, we walked a long way together, and in a small country, you have to still face the people who you find difficult, because we are all sort of trapped in here together."

I don't know if that's right, but maybe I don't have to have an opinion about every single thing on earth, and maybe I'm not here to find out the truth about myself or my illness or my mother or anything else but to accept that I never will. Honestly, all I want right now is to live in a normal house with one of those things in the refrigerator that dispenses ice. And what about people from high school? What are they doing? Having expensive weddings. Working in offices. Decorating their houses. Is that so bad?

I FIND PAVLA lying in the gazebo. I sit in a hammock close to her. She asks how my night was. I tell her it was hard but good. I ask about hers.

"I kept seeing myself, things I am doing, and I was vomiting from how I am," she says. "I said I will never do it again, and the answer came to me, *You will.*"

I nod to show her I can relate. I hope she doesn't think I'm agreeing that she will.

"Mája, please, can we have peace?" she says.

"You're the one who said you were never going to speak to me again."

"I want Kubík to be happy," she says. "And I see that you are making him happy, but now I know from Claire that it was not making you happy."

"What did she tell you?"

"She told me you have a hard time with Kubík. Not many details, but I know what it means. He asked me not to tell you about me and him, but I see now I should have told you everything the first night we met."

"He should have told me."

"I know I am not an easy person," she says. "I was still suffering from our story."

She probably only wants to have peace with me so she can be in touch with him again, but for now I don't mind. And I do like her. I remember what I thought when I first met her. She's strange, and I like her. At least she's honest.

WHEN KUBA COMES, for once I don't feel those hooks pulling him away to be elsewhere adored.

"How was it?" I ask.

"I think it was last time."

"Why?"

"I realised it's like having a window open for a second, and you remember the view, but you don't know how to open the window yourself, and I don't want to spend my whole life looking out of the windows."

It reminds me of The Lady of Shalott. *I'm half sick of shadows.*

"What happened?"

"I had the message that I can't be the dance leader any more," he says. "It's impossible to imagine, but it was so clear. I try to argue with that. I said I don't want to transform the lineage, but I feel like it's my mission, and the answer was very calming. It was, *Why would you spend your time with cultivating something what you don't trust in any more?*"

"I never thought I would say this, but the dances actually helped me a lot," I say. "I think they helped you, too."

"I saw Otto in the night," he says. "I asked if I can see him as he is now, but he said, *You would not understand. Be grateful it's like it is.* Then I saw terrible things. I saw the wars, and the tortures, and destroyed cities, and the rainforest burning down. It was so bad. I saw that we are killing our planet and we are killing each other. And when the visions stopped I was still crying, and Dante came, and he put the tobacco into my eyes, and when I open my eyes again I saw everyone else is gone, and it's only me and him in the room, and I told him what I saw, and I asked him what am I supposed to do? Like is it more important to be the activist and try to change it, or am I supposed to believe those spiritual books saying I'm supposed to work on my own inner integrity. And he told me everything what I saw in my visions was a picture of what's inside of me."

"So are we supposed to do nothing about how fucked up the world is?"

"I think it means we are supposed to know and acknowledge all our parts," he says. "Even our worst shits. So we can transform it and find the peaceful place where we can love and act for the good of all."

He takes my hands. "Májenka, I thought I was bringing the salvation to my nation. But now I know that even if I feel like I can die from sadness from leaving my homeland, it can be, and it will be okay."

THE FIRE WALKING ceremony is the final thing before I leave. It's Kuba's gift to me. I read up on how it works, to make sure I won't end up scarred for life. It sounds like it doesn't burn you because wood and feet are not good heat conductors, and the period of contact between them is brief. So walk quickly, I guess.

I leave for New Zealand in two days. I've signed up for a ten-day meditation course with Gina. It was my idea. She goes every year, and the timing worked out perfectly. I expect to be totally falling apart when I get there, so that will be a good motivation to finally learn to meditate. At the very least it will save me from having to talk to anyone about my stupid problems.

Kuba is going to wrap up his work and scatter Otto's ashes in the forest with Sophie and some other friends before he goes to New Mexico. When he's finished there, he's planning to join me. Barbora, his past-life mother, called his present-life mother and told him she has to stop him and he's betraying the Czech Republic. Honestly, I'm not counting on him coming. I'm not counting on anything any more.

The ceremony is going to be led by the guy who told me he was Tesco and Kuba was Penny Market. We meet in a big room in a farmhouse outside of Prague. I look around to see if I can figure out who Kuba's special woman will be, but there's no one obvious.

A talking stone is passed around the circle. When it's my turn, I say, "Ja jsem Mája, ja jsem z Kanady, a rozumím trochu česky." I have learned something here after all.

When a woman with red hair is introducing herself, Kuba says, "Tesco wants this one."

"How do you know?"

"I observe it."

She speaks briefly and passes the stone on. The next person is about to start, but Tesco interrupts.

"What did he say?" I ask.

"He said she didn't say the most important part, but that's her decision," Kuba says.

The woman asks to have the stone back, and she continues. "She says last night he was healing her," Kuba says. "He was sitting with her and touching her, and then they were holding each other, and when she woke up in the morning she saw the sky, and she felt this is how we are supposed to live, because he was teaching her that women have to show men how to treat them, and men have to show women how to treat them."

He looks very proud of himself. "Isn't he married?" I whisper.

"He is going to New Zealand this year," Kuba says. "So next time we see him he will be dragging huge pounamu behind him, teaching haka."

When the sharing is over, the red-haired woman speaks to Kuba excitedly but doesn't look at me. I don't understand what they're saying, but I can feel what's going on between them as clearly as if it was written in lights on their foreheads. He reaches into my bag of dried mango. I want to slap his hands, because I know what he's going to do. He eats a piece and holds one out to her. She eats it from his hand.

I believe I could be totally compassionate and loving if people could stop being such motherfucking assholes.

WE'RE SUPPOSED TO meet in pairs and talk about what we want to burn in the fire. Someone asks that woman if she will speak to me, and she says, "No, I don't want to speak English."

I end up with Tesco. I tell him I want to burn my anger and judgment but keep my discernment.

"What is discernment?" he asks.

"It's like judgment, but without emotion. Critical thinking?"

"It's better if you burn all," he says. "Anger, judgment, everything."

"I can't," I say. "I mean I don't want to."

"You're idealistic," he says. "That's not bad in itself, but you have to learn to trust. Otherwise you take all the responsibility on yourself, and you can never relax. If you give the responsibility back to others by trusting them, you can live in peace."

I hate the way he's trying to teach me, but maybe he's right. I tell him I'll think about it. Then he kisses me on the mouth, and I'm so shocked that I freeze and do nothing. "Sometimes it's good to focus on the positives," he says. "There is so much to criticise."

KUBA PLAYS ME a song I haven't heard before. I ask him what it's about.

"It's about the death," he says. "Before the body goes to the church, the soul is telling the body that you didn't care of me at all because you were having so many needs and so many enjoyments, and the soul is blaming the body like that through whole song, but then in the last verse the body answers, *Don't blame me soul. For all of what you said, you were with me.*"

"Who wrote it?" I ask.

"It is made by people," he says. "There is no author."

I have a nap and dream I'm at my book launch. There are so many people. Someone gives me a copy of my book. The cover is a picture of my mother wearing an orange shirt. When I start to read, I realise it isn't my book at all. I decide I should keep going, because I don't want to embarrass everyone, but the organiser interrupts me. She says she's so sorry, but the real author has arrived, and she mixed up the rooms. She leads me to another room, which has hundreds of chairs set up, all of them empty.

People are making hooting noises, and there's smoke rising from behind the farmhouse. I've decided not to burn my anger on the fire, because just the thought of that man telling me to do it makes me want to burn this whole place down.

I wonder if it would have changed anything if my mother had allowed herself be as angry as I am. Somehow I lost the handkerchief she gave me. If I had it, I would bury it with her. She left this country running away from something, but I hope that when she stepped over the border she was running toward something, too. I'd like to think it was the same when she left me. I hope she pictured a better life for herself, even if I wasn't in it.

IN THE FIELD, they've made a huge fire next to an enormous linden tree. They put down a red carpet to show us how to walk across the coals. "You have to look forward, not to your feet," Kuba translates. "Know your intention and walk to that but not looking down, looking ahead."

People are throwing what they want to burn into the fire. Some make a big performance of it. They dance and drum. Many of them are naked. Tesco is hopping around the fire with his massive drum, his penis flapping, and I laugh to myself, because it seems so absurd—not just the situation, but how life-and-death important it has all become for me.

Kuba and Tesco use shovels to rake coals from the fire and throw them into a path on the ground. When the coal carpet is prepared, they walk across it one at a time.

Kuba is naked. I wish he wasn't. That woman is naked too, and gyrating by the fire. Kuba drums as he walks across. I'm next. I forget everything. I take a step and it burns. I take another step, and it burns. I run. At the end, Kuba is waiting to hug me.

"You were watching the ground the whole time!" he says. "Are you burned?"

He says it will help if I walk in the wet grass. I go out beyond the firelight, work my toes into the cool dirt, and watch the others from the darkness. From here, this scene could be ancient. Human figures dancing and drumming around a fire. And here I am alone on the periphery. But I'm not alone.

I close my eyes and feel the drums through the earth, and I know there's a presence out here with me. I think it's always been with me. I don't know who or what it is, but I know I'm not alone, and I'm not afraid.

Back at the fire, Kuba asks if I want to walk over the coals again. I assume he's joking. "I will wait for you on the end," he says. "You can watch me."

This time I look straight ahead, not at Kuba, but past him, and it doesn't burn.

Autumn

I SPEND A lot of time thinking about lunch. What will it be? Will I get there in time for salad? Some of the others are motivated. They line up outside the dining room door to wait for the gong. Gina is one of them.

In the meditation hall, I spend most of my time fighting sleep by planning the lasagna I'm going to make when I get to Gina's house. It goes like this: red sauce, pasta, white sauce, lentils, red sauce, pasta, white sauce, eggplant, red sauce, pasta, white sauce, pasta, red sauce, cheese. It's not what I'm supposed to be doing, obviously, but it keeps me awake and my mind off my back.

I would never have guessed that sitting still could be like perching on nails if you do it long enough. I asked for a back rest, but the student teacher talked me out of it. I think pain is part of the process.

When the gong goes, I slowly stand, go outside, put on my shoes, and walk to the dining room. I never waste any time doing this, but I don't rush, either. The salad is almost always gone by the time I get there.

GOENKA, THE TEACHER, is dead, so we listen to his voice through speakers and watch videos of his talks in the evening. His wife is sitting beside him in the videos. You see her at the beginning, then it zooms in on him, but sometimes you can still see the edge of her shadow. I wonder if she's loving and supporting him, or if she's thinking, *They have no idea how you really are.* Most likely she's focusing on the sensations above her upper lip, as I should be.

I have opinions about everyone here, even though I've never spoken to most of them. The one I have the most opinions about is Gina's blonde dance camp friend. I find her intolerable, even in silence. Her clothes, the way she walks, the fact that she always looks like she's been crying. Even her shoes annoy me when I see them outside the hall, all helter skelter and in the way.

The instructions are over, the hall goes quiet. I manage a few seconds of focusing on the triangular area under my nose before I'm imagining Kuba in New Mexico with his soul lover. I open my eyes and steal a glance at Never Moving Man. When I arrive in the hall, that guy is always in his place, and when I leave, he is in exactly the same position. Even during the evening talks he sits like that. He never moves.

I want Kuba. I'm so angry with him for not being who I wanted him to be. He will be starting his silent retreat now. It's been four days since we last spoke. I was already in New Zealand when he told me about the silent retreat. I asked him if anyone he knew was going with him, and he said no, but I knew that his soul lover was going to be travelling with him from the dance retreat. After that, he didn't write for three days. Then he wrote and said he's afraid I'm leaving him because not only can I have no assurance about his abilities to live outside of the Czech Republic, but also he's an irresponsible jerk.

I was staying with my father's family. I couldn't justify being in Auckland and not seeing them. I was sleeping in my oldest half-sister's room because she was away on a school trip.

There's nothing in there except a bare mattress and sleeping bag. Apparently she hasn't accepted living in this country.

Every time I managed to speak to Kuba on Skype, I got some disturbing new piece of information. He told me that woman from fire walking was calling him a lot. She told him she thinks they would make a perfect couple, and she gave him a stone and a photograph of herself. He acts so surprised, as if he hadn't orchestrated the whole thing.

The day before I left my father's house, Kuba was supposed to call me in the afternoon, which was his evening in New Mexico. At six p.m., I tried to call him, but he didn't answer. I knew something was wrong. From thousands of miles away, I could feel it. I went to sleep with the phone by my head, and at eleven p.m. I woke up in a panic. It was four in the morning where he was. I tried to call his cellphone again. He didn't answer, so I called again. And again. The third time, he picked up. "Hello, my love," he said.

"Why didn't you call me?"

"Sorry, lásko," he said. "It was so difficult circumstances. There was a storm, and the marquee was damaged, and then my programme was delayed, and after I stepped on a nail."

"You're lying."

"I am not lying."

"You're leaving something out. Are you with your soul lover?"

"Who?"

"Gemma!" I hate saying their names, and I hate that I remember them all.

"Yes, she is here."

"And is she the reason you didn't call me?"

There was a long pause. "Lásko, it is middle of the night."

"Tell me what happened, Kuba."

"Okay, you are true," he says. "After the programme, we gave each other a hug for a goodnight, but it was getting really

231

long, and she was making some sounds and doing some movements, and I started to feel physically excited, so it was clear that
this can turn very quickly into very wild physical connection.
I managed to sneak out of the hug and just bow to her and say
goodnight and go to bed. And I needed to take a time to breathe
through it because it was bit shocking, because I don't want these
things to be happening more, and I saw I am still inviting it, so
I just needed few moments to put myself together before I call
you, and then I fell asleep."

"Why are you like this?" I shouted. I didn't care who heard
me. "I want you to please, please, please, get out of my life. You're
poison!"

He was saying, "Lásko, lásko, lásko . . ."

When it was over, I lay on the bare mattress and wailed. My
father came in. I hated him seeing me like that, but I couldn't
stop. He sat next to me and put his hand on my back. Then all
my rage turned on him. I screamed and swore, told him he was
a worthless piece of shit useless father, and he killed my mother,
and I hated him. His youngest daughter came in and held her
hands over his ears, and I fell back onto the mattress and cried.
He picked up his girl, pulled the sleeping bag over me, and left.
When he came back, my teeth were chattering. He sat down on
the bed. I felt so cold and tired of everything.

"She didn't want me," I said.

"That's not true," he said. "We both wanted children."

I wiped the snot from my face and looked at him. "She didn't
want *me*. *You* didn't want *me*."

"My darling," he said. "It wasn't about you at all."

You can tell the truth because it reaches your heart. She was
lost in her own story, and so was he.

And so am I.

In the morning, no one mentioned my outburst. My dad
made me fresh orange juice, and I took it to the sunroom and did

the crossword. When Gina came to get me, late as always, I told her I didn't want to talk, so she talked the whole way.

When we got here, there was a rush to put our valuables in safe-keeping, get our room keys, and organise our bedding before the orientation. We just had time for a cup of tea before the course started. That blonde woman sat next to me, and she and Gina talked over everyone. Apparently she went to Gina for a palm reading and Gina encouraged her to go to dance camp, where she met the man of her dreams.

"It's a case of the universe sending me the perfect green man who is compassionate and striving to change the world in the eco and human rights sense," she said. The men were filing into the room for the orientation. "And he has chickens and so many qualities I was asking for in a man." Everyone else had gone quiet, but she didn't lower her voice. "Like someone who's real and who wants to help me to build my studio and who cares about the environment and the ocean, but I'm afraid he will run away from me because I told him about my sad divorce."

After the orientation, the men went to their side of the complex, and I said goodbye to Gina. "You know you're not allowed to communicate with me during the course," I said.

"I don't want to communicate with you," she said.

"Good," I said, although I was actually terrified of being alone with my thoughts for so long.

She's already broken the no-communication rule. Today she winked at me when we passed each other in the toilets. I know because I saw her in the mirror when I looked away.

GINA STARTLES WHEN she sees me on my bed. She puts a bag by my feet and leaves. Inside the bag I find a sweater, a scarf, and an extra hot water bottle. I would prefer if she would follow the rules, but then again, I have been cold.

I've devised a sling chair that's reasonably comfortable.

I stack three cushions under me, wrap one of the blankets tightly around myself, and tuck the ends in under the cushions so when I lean back it sort of supports me. I try to follow the technique as described. I get lost in thought. I come back. I start to nod off. I squeeze my hands. My back hurts. I move. I get lost in thought. I come back. I do this again and again. I try to be patient with myself. I'm not getting anywhere, but I mind less, so that's something.

In the evening talks, Goenka describes what we are privately experiencing so perfectly that we have to laugh, because we're all in the same monstrous predicament. He talks about devotional, intellectual, and experiential wisdom. I get the theory, and I understand that at some point I have to make the leap from theory to practice, but until now, I've never been given such clear instructions. After all my fretting over what I'm supposed to do, here's an answer: focus on the triangular space between your nose and upper lip.

TODAY WE LEARNED Vipassana. I thought the triangular area thing was it, but that was to prepare us by sharpening our awareness. Now we're scanning our bodies from the tops of our heads to the tips of our toes, observing gross and subtle sensations and then moving on without reacting.

I start at the top of my head, but before I manage to notice anything there I'm distracted by the stabbing pain in my lower back. I start again from the top of my head and stay there until I feel my blood pulsing in my scalp, then I'm back to my pain. I'm sure my spine will snap if I don't move. It's impossible to think about anything else. It occurs to me that this is how my mother must have felt most of the time. But I can stop it by changing position. For her, there was nowhere to go.

I try again. I bring my attention to the top of my head, wait to feel the pulse there, move to the back of my head, stay there until I feel a tickle on my skin. Then forehead, eyes, nose, mouth, chin, neck. When I get to my back, the pain is so intense that I have to lean forward and put my head on the floor. I observe the pain until it eases, then I sit up and try to continue, but it happens again, and I lean forward and fall asleep until a server tugs on my blanket.

When I go back to my room, the towel I hung up outside has been straightened, and three more pegs have been added.

AT TEATIME, I watch Gina sitting outside on the balcony. Her mouth is moving. I bet she's winning an argument in her head. I send her a telepathic message that I love her. I can't remember the last time I told her that. This whole time I've been obsessing over Kuba, and there's my darling aunt, her beautiful eyes. She's an old lady now. And she's been such a good friend to me.

I feel so nostalgic. I want to gather my photos around me and listen to Leonard Cohen. I thought I was ahead of Kuba, because I'm not attached to things like he is, but now I think maybe you have to be attached first for letting go to have any meaning.

I go to my room and cry for a long time. It's so touching to imagine how many people in my life already knew the things I thought I was discovering but let me figure them out for myself.

I remember how Drew's lips quivered when he cried. All I saw was need. I'm sorry. I didn't understand love then, and I still don't.

AT LUNCH, a bowl of salad appears next to my plate. I decide to save it for last, but before I can eat it, Gina's hand swoops in to take it back. She must have thought I was rejecting it. I find it annoying, but also adorable. She's just not a rule follower, my aunt.

TODAY WAS VERY dark. Stomachache and profound post-event rumination, but not about one event, about my whole life and personality. The main theme is how I've used people by seeing them as characters. I've interviewed people in terrible situations, and when they shared their stories with me I thought, *yes, gold.* Even Kuba. How much of our relationship was me studying him? I feel horrible about that.

I also feel generally useless and not nice and trapped in my narrow worldview. I hate that I'm so self-righteous, and I judge everyone, like that poor blonde friend of Gina's. And Drew's parents. I thought them cutting me off proved they didn't care about me, but now I think it proves they cared much more than I did. And I hate that I'm not perfect. I'm so scared people will notice how self-absorbed I am and how wrong my thoughts are and judge me the way I judge everything. And the arrogance of imagining that I have to be perfect and from a position of perfection offer my compassion and forgiveness to others. What ignorance. I feel like I'm full of tar. And still my stupid brain, which can't shut up for even a second, tells me I am very noble for judging myself this way.

Usually I call Becca to talk me down when I'm obsessing. She would say, "Realistically, will you be thinking about this in a week? A month? So why don't you drop it now and do something else with your day." But there's nothing else *to* do here, and nowhere to hide from myself.

GINA VISITS ME in my dream. *Having a nice time?* she asks.

"What am I supposed to do?"

Love, she says.

"Who? Kuba? It's too hard!"

Just love.

I wake up, and the rumination resumes, along with the stabbing stomach pains. I can't escape this self-torture, and now the torture itself is piled on the growing heap of my shortcomings, because it's just more self-obsession.

Since I have nowhere else to go, I try going toward the part of myself I'm so disgusted by—the part that wants to hide, that wants too much to be seen, that feels weird and embarrassing, that feels superior and self-righteous, that wants to have a formula for everything, to arrive and know. I get close to her and tell her I don't know how to love her yet, but I'm going to try to stop hurting her.

GOENKA IS DRIVING me bananas with repeating himself. He names sensations for like an hour every time. "May be a prickling sensation, a tickling sensation, a sensation of heat, a sensation of cold . . ." I want to scream, "Stop naming sensations!" I just feel like *enough*. I want to be healthy and have a career, and a home, and a family, the end.

When he finally leaves us to scan our bodies, I'm determined not to get lost in my thoughts or dwell on my pain or fall asleep. I start at the top of my head. My back hurts. I move to the back of my head, my forehead, my face. When I get to my legs, I realise that my back stopped hurting at some point, but as I move up from my feet, the pain resumes. I breathe and keep scanning. At the top of my head, the pain has stopped again, but on the way down my chest it intensifies. I keep going down to my hips, my legs, my feet and toes, then back up. On the way up, I stop at my back again and observe the pain, and I see that I am *in* pain, and there's a part of me that hates it and wants to get out and another part that's observing it and doesn't want anything.

I start at the top of my head again, notice, move, notice, move. I make it to my chest, my stomach, down my legs to my feet, my toes, then I start going back up again, and when I get to my back I notice that there is still pain, but it's like I'm behind it, and then there's a state that, I don't know what to call it. Vibrations?

A voice is saying, *You're doing it!* Then the voice goes away, and when the chanting starts, it echoes through me.

I remember Mabit saying *Jacques is not important* until the snake released him. I try it. *Mája is not important. Mája is not important. Mája is not important.* A jolt of pain shoots up my back. This is what I'm working on now. Before it was Kuba, now it's back pain. What's the difference? We have wars, betray each other, defile nature and our own souls because we want to feel some things and not feel other things.

EVERY TIME I recognise myself in one of Goenka's stories about how people are, I think I won't do that again. Then I remember what ayahuasca told Pavla. *You will.*

I accidentally smuggled *The Unbearable Lightness of Being* into my room. I found it in the top pocket of my suitcase. I won't read it, but it's comforting to know that it's there.

I want chocolate and a hot bath. Never Moving Man will probably miss out on having a family and career because he's so focused on being enlightened. I wonder if he's thought that through.

Should I stay here? Or go back to Czech? Should I give up on writing and do comms work again? Or train to be something else? Should I be with Kuba? Should I leave him? Find someone I can do crosswords with? The answer comes to me. *It doesn't matter.*

I wish I felt like I felt yesterday. Another craving. I thought I was making progress. Now I'm back to my thinking parties. It goes like this: scanning, hoping for the vibrations, pain, guilt, boredom, lasagna, skin (that's back), worry, pain, trying to get back to the vibrations, falling asleep, pain, acceptance, little insight, scanning, sort of vibrations, not wanting it to end, pain, lasagna, frustration, falling asleep.

I FEEL A softening in me. I've stopped trying to meditate. I wish I'd thought of it sooner. Instead, I lie awake in the dark and have conversations with the new voice in my head. It's very helpful. I ask if I can accept myself as I am. *Yes.* Can I accept the people I love? *Yes.* What about the people I hate? *Yes.* Why do I judge everything? *To be safe.* Does it make me safe? *Nothing can make you safe, because you are already safe, and you always have been.* How is that possible? *Everything you experience is an opportunity to let go.*

WHEN THE FINAL sitting is over, the student teachers leave without a word. No long hugs. In fact, we're not supposed to touch at all, but Gina bursts out of the meditation hall and grabs me, and I squeeze her back.

I'm not ready to talk to people yet, so I go back to my room and finish *The Unbearable Lightness of Being.* I feel like it was written only for me. Near the end, the narrator talks about the thread that ties us to the Garden of Eden, where Adam stared at his reflection in the water with the mute incomprehension of an animal. What I wonder is if that thread isn't only pulling us back but also drawing us toward a paradise we can never regain, not because it doesn't exist, but because we can't go there as ourselves.

The dining hall is so loud, and everyone is lovely and totally different than I imagined. The blonde woman, whose name is Lori, tells me her new boyfriend is picking her up, as if that reveals something important about their relationship. "He's so kind," she says. "That's all I want now. Kindness."

She asks me if I have a boyfriend and how we met, so I tell her the magical story.

"It was the same with my ex-husband," she says. "I was working as an escort, and he was a client, and we just had a connection, like we knew each other forever."

I regret not being more honest. She asks how I found the course.

"It was hard," I say. "I felt bad about myself a lot of the time."

"Me too," she says. "I've been feeling so guilty. Like having really negative thoughts, and I couldn't stop them. I didn't think it would be like that."

"How did you think it would be?"

"Peaceful? You?"

"I guess I thought I might come to terms with the void? Stop avoiding it?"

"I kept thinking about all the bad things I put myself through," she says. "How I don't connect with my family, and how I lied and cheated and stole." We sit in silence for a while, then she says, "But now I feel better."

"Me too."

"You know," she says, "You seem to be really sophisticated and smart and everything, but when I first saw you I felt like you're not in touch with yourself." I feel like crying. She pats my arm. "But you're a good person," she says. "And I know I'm a good person. People will forgive us."

I'M DRIVING TO Gina's house. She's gone to a retreat with Lori and her boyfriend. About half an hour from the centre, I hit reception and my phone starts to ding. I pull over and open Gmail. I expect there to be lots of emails from Kuba, but there's only one.

Beloved Májenka,

While you are reading this probably you just finished the silence. I hope that was a rich time for you, lásko.

I feel so bad for the pain I caused so many people. Especially you. I was imprisoned by my fear of losing. That's what our partnership was about. From the first night, you saw it. Attachments. To you. My country. My mission. My fame.

Where I was for the retreat there was a river, and big part of the day I was watching, so soon I knew every detail of that part of that river. Every rock and every curve, where each creature was sleeping. But then one night there was a storm, and the next day when I looked it was all different. And all those beings what lives there have to count that it can happen hundreds of times in the life. And even old cultures, where it's sure that this is how it is, and it always was this way, somewhere it started, and somewhere it will end, and after the storm, when the river changes, people will have to make new structures and new possibilities to get attached.

I'm sorry it took so long time. It was that so exciting moment when I felt like the world is opening and you were like fucking open world, let's close it. But I see now how big gift it is for me, and the guidance came back to me, and I saw that I have to give up everything. My attachments to my country, to other women, to any subculture, any belonging. And I have to do it not for you, but for myself.

I am at Auckland. If you wish to see me, I can come to you wherever you are. If you do not contact me, I will not try to contact you more.

Miluju Tě,
Jakub

I have an instant headache. I want to call him. I need to hear again that we are indivisible and he will never, ever leave me. I need to ask him how can he give up, after everything I went through for him. But I know that's not true. I didn't do anything for him. I did it for myself. And it isn't him that I can't give up, but the way he saw me. Now he's letting me off the hook, which means I have to choose, and either way, when everything settles, I'll have to start again.

I STOP AT a mall to get one of those fluorescent ice blocks I used to like when I was a kid. I'm so stunned by the lights and sounds that I have a hard time finding the New World, and I have to sit on a bench to get my bearings.

Watching the other shoppers, I'm reminded of the carp in the pond by Kuba and Otto's house. When Kuba was away, I used to sit and watch people fishing there. I remember thinking that everything about it was fake—the pond was artificial, the fish were farmed. But they were real fish, and no doubt completely real to themselves, as you could see when they were pulled up to the surface to die.

I assume most of us in this mall understand our situation about as well as those carp understand Christmas, and yet little by little, each in our own way, we're coming home to the truth sleeping in our hearts.

I'm at the checkout when my phone dings again. It's Kuba: *Can I ask you one question?*

I see it so clearly. I'll answer him, and we'll dive back into our story until we're ready to do things differently, separately or together. At least now it feels like a choice. And whatever his question is, I know the answer.

THANK YOU

To the Canada Council for the Arts, and to everyone at Freehand, especially Debbie Willis and Kelsey Attard for their unwavering patience and support.

To my early readers and otherways supporters—Emily, Jean, Martha, Martina, Matěj, Max, Michael, MK, Naďa, Odette, Peter, Rebecca, Sara, Susan, Václav, and Yvette.

To Dr. Jacques Mabit and Dr. Rosa Give Nakazawa. The interviews that Mája watches, and her conversation with Dr. Mabit, are based on excerpts from interviews I conducted with Dr. Mabit in 2013 and 2014, which are used in this context with permission.

For their generous help with various aspects of my research, thank you to Pavla Drengubáková, Dušan Drbohlav, Jiří Dynda, Helena Dyndová, Pavel Horák, Te Ataahia Hurihanganui, Zuzana Jurková, Tomáš Kočko, Tomáš Kotrlý, Jan A. Kozák, Zdeněk R. Nešpor, Ivana Noble, and Dáša Rohelová.

To Jaromír Nohavica and Vlasta Redl for permitting me to reference their work, and to Marlen Kryl for her permission to quote a verse from "Děkuji," by Karel Kryl, as translated by Lily Sekytova in Josef Císařovský's documentary *Čas hanby mlčení naděje*.

The book Mája picks up at Pieter and June's house is *Supernatural*, by Graham Hancock. "Whatever the question, love is the answer" is a quote from *Everyday Wisdom*, by Dr. Wayne W. Dyer (Hay House, Inc. Carlsbad, CA. 2005. p. 23). The quote that begins, "The people of this world are like the three butterflies in front of a candle's flame" is from Sufi poet Farīd al-Dīn 'Aṭṭār. The book Mája reads from at random in a restaurant is *Zen Heart, Zen Mind* by Ama Samy, quoted with permission from Father Samy.

My sincere gratitude to Dhamma Medini Vipassasa Meditation Centre in Kaukapakapa.

And to my family. Na věky věků.

DISCOGRAPHY

The following are the songs mentioned, in the order they appear.

The epigraph is from "Lásko, milá lásko," traditional, as performed by Hradišťan.

The song Kuba sings to Mája at dance camp shortly after they meet is "Přijdu hned," written and performed by Vlasta Redl.

Mája's favourite song is "Kometa," written and performed by Jaromír Nohavica.

The list of songs Mája requests from Kuba includes "V půl osmé," written and performed by Vlasta Redl, Jaroslav Samson Lenk, and Slávek Janoušek, "Nad stádem koní," written and performed by Buty, and "Slunovrat," written and performed by Brontosauři.

The song Mája remembers her mother singing to her is the Czech national anthem, "Kde domov můj," written by František Škroup and Josef Kajetán Tyl.

The lyrics Pavla sends to Kuba when Mája and Kuba are at Nohavica's concert are from "Jakube, Jakube," written and performed by Jaromír Nohavica.

When she's reflecting on belief in the future, Mája refers to "Těšínská," written and performed by Jaromír Nohavica.

The song Kuba plays for Otto on piano, which Mája says opens the sadness of centuries, is "Lieskovsků dolinů," traditional lyrics, music by Bezobratři.

After Mája ignores him and reads her book on the floor, Kuba sings "Pocestný," text by František Ladislav Čelakovský, music by Alois Jelen, as performed by Spirituál Kvintet.

At the Museum of Communism, Mája hears the song "Děkuji," written and performed by Karel Kryl, in Josef Císařovský's documentary *Čas hanby mlčení naděje*.

At fire walking, Kuba sings Mája "A když bylo před kostelem," traditional, as performed by Tomáš Kočko ("Moravská").

ALSO BY CATHERINE COOPER

The Western Home
White Elephant